THAT EMPTY FEELING

PETER CORRIS is known as the 'godfather' of Australian crime fiction through his Cliff Hardy detective stories. He has written in many other areas, including a co-authored autobiography of the late Professor Fred Hollows, a history of boxing in Australia, spy novels, historical novels and a collection of short stories about golf (see www.petercorris. net). In 1999, Peter Corris was awarded the Lifetime Achievement Award from the Crime Writers Association of Australia and, in 2009, the Ned Kelly Award for Best Fiction for *Deep Water*. He is married to writer Jean Bedford and has lived in Sydney for most of his life. They have three daughters and six grandsons.

Peter Corris's Cliff Hardy novels include *The Empty Beach*, *Master's Mates*, *The Coast Road*, *Saving Billie*, *The Undertow*, *Appeal Denied*, *The Big Score*, *Open File*, *Deep Water*, *Torn Apart*, *Follow the Money*, *Comeback*, *The Dunbar Case*, *Silent Kill* and *Gun Control*. *That Empty Feeling* is his forty-first Cliff Hardy book.

He writes a regular weekly column for the online journal *Newtown Review of Books* (www.newtownreviewofbooks. com.au).

PETER CORRIS

THAT EMPTY FEELING

ALLEN&UNWIN

SYDNEY • MELBOURNE • AUCKLAND • LONDON

Thanks to Jean Bedford, Miriam Corris,
Tom Kelly, Jo Jarrah and Angela Handley.

First published in 2016

Copyright © Peter Corris 2016

Allen & Unwin
83 Alexander Street
Crows Nest NSW 2065
Australia
Phone: (61 2) 8425 0100
Email: info@allenandunwin.com
Web: www.allenandunwin.com

Cataloguing-in-Publication details are available
from the National Library of Australia
www.trove.nla.gov.au

ISBN 978 1 76011 207 3

Internal design by Emily O'Neill
Set in 12/17 pt Adobe Caslon by Midland Typesetters, Australia
Printed and bound in Australia by Griffin Press

10 9 8 7 6 5 4 3 2 1

MIX
Paper from
responsible sources
FSC® C009448

The paper in this book is FSC® certified.
FSC® promotes environmentally responsible,
socially beneficial and economically viable
management of the world's forests.

To the memory of my parents,
Thomas Corris (1913–1967)
and Joan Kelly Corris (1913–2013)

Hell is empty, and all the devils are here.
　　　　　　　　—William Shakespeare, *The Tempest*

part one

1

I was sitting on the balcony of my daughter Megan's flat turning over the pages of the *Sydney Morning Herald* and trying to decide if I liked its new tabloid format. They called it a 'compact' but I prefer to call a spade a spade.

I decided I didn't care one way or the other—the paper was mostly gossip and stories that didn't matter much now and wouldn't matter at all tomorrow. I turned to the obituary page and almost dropped the paper.

'Shit!'

Megan appeared at the sliding door. 'What now? They're bringing back the death penalty?'

'Barry Bartlett's dead.'

'Who's Barry Bartlett?'

I gazed out at Camperdown Park across the street. It was mid-morning in early spring; all the benches were occupied and people were sprawled on the grass, some already unwrapping their lunches. Barry had always enjoyed his lunch.

'It's a long story,' I said.

Megan came out and eased herself into one of the cane chairs. She was eight months pregnant. It hadn't been planned but she was happy about it. So was her partner Hank and their son Ben, my grandson. Ben was five and looked a lot like me—tall and dark with a hooked nose and a low hairline. He wanted a sister and you'd have to hope that if she came along she'd look like her mother rather than her grandad. Megan, in her late thirties, still turns heads. She looks a bit like Sigourney Weaver with a few more kilos.

'Cliff,' she said, 'Ben's in school, I've done the housework, prepared our lunch and I reckon it's just about time for a drink. I've got nothing to do until 3.30. I wouldn't mind a story.'

Megan's partner is an American. She's picked up expressions like 'in school' and they watch gridiron on television. She ran her hands over her swollen belly.

'Sure it's not twins?'

They'd decided they didn't want to be told the sex of the child but they knew they weren't getting twins.

'It's not fucking twins, as you well know. Just a big lump like Ben—and you, probably. What were you when you were born?'

'Nine pounds something, I believe. Don't blame me. Hank's a bit bigger than I am.'

Megan groaned. 'I can see the stretch marks. I'll get you a beer and you can tell me all about Barry what's-his-name. Take my mind off thoughts of the delivery suite.'

She brought the beer and I drank most of the stubby before saying anything. Megan looked enquiringly at me.

'What?'

'It's not something I like to think about.'

'Not your finest hour?'

'Not by a long shot. I opened a file on it but in the end I didn't put anything much in it. I just left it pretty empty. Empty . . . the whole thing had an empty feeling.'

'Probably do you good to get it off your chest.'

2

Barry Bartlett was what the media called 'a colourful Sydney identity', which means that he was a crook who had stayed out of gaol for more than twenty-five years. His English family had migrated to Australia just after the Second World War—Ronald and Irene Bartlett, Barry, his sister Milly and his brother George. Barry was in his early teens then.

'I was a terror on that ship and no mistake,' he told me.

This was close to thirty years later, when I first knew him. He'd been a Balmain tearaway who'd left school early, worked for bookies and light-fingered wharfies and done eighteen months in Long Bay for assault with menaces in his late teens. Nothing since. He'd branched out into big-time fencing, illegal gambling and nightclub ownership. He also managed a few boxers. An Aboriginal fighter I knew, Bobby Munday, introduced us.

Bobby went on to have a successful career and have his money honestly managed and invested by Bartlett, which was a very rare thing then and since. I sat with Bartlett at a few of Bobby's fights. After we watched him just squeak a points decision defending his Commonwealth welterweight title, Bartlett phoned me.

'That cunt Simmonds wants to buy Bobby's contract and put him in against Sugar Ray Leonard in Vegas.'

'Jesus,' I said.

'Bobby's not in that class and never was, plus he's near the top of the hill if not fucking over it, wouldn't you say?'

'Yeah.'

'I know you've got influence with him, Hardy. I won't sell his contract but those things aren't really worth a pinch of shit. Simmonds could find a lawyer to get Bobby out of it. There'd be one hell of a big pay night and Simmonds and the lawyer and some fat prick in the US'd get the lion's share and Bobby'd end up with brain damage or worse. I want you to convince him not to do it.'

'A lot of money to pass up.'

'He's got a lot of fucking money.'

This was well before the days of email. Bartlett had the accountant he'd put in charge of Bobby's affairs fax me over details of Bobby's bank accounts, investments and tax status. As things stood, Bobby was set for life, with enough coming in from investments to live on and capital to invest in other enterprises of his own choosing. His life and that of his wife were insured; there were tax-friendly trusts set up for his two kids.

I phoned Bartlett. 'I should have had you manage me.'

Bartlett laughed. 'Bobby had some big fights at the right time. That's how he got the world ranking. I wrung money out of the fucking media every time they wanted him to say two words. That doco brought in a motza. What's the most you ever made from a case?'

'Okay, point taken, but you know fighters. They don't know when it's over and they don't like to be told.'

'I'm asking for your help. Might sound fucking weird, but I'm proud of what I've done for that boy. Makes me feel I've given something back to this country that's been so good to me.'

I laughed. 'Blarney—I thought you were a Pom, not a Mick.'

'Call it what you like. I'll pay you . . .'

'Shut up, you're not getting the bloody moral drop on me. I'll do what I can. The last thing I want to see is Bobby on the canvas in Las Vegas and Teddy Simmonds counting the money.'

I rang Bobby and asked if he could spare me some time. Me being a private detective amused him, and he was usually pleased to see me to talk boxing and make jokes about trench coats and .38s. Didn't matter that I didn't own a trench coat and my Smith & Wesson hadn't seen the light of day for quite a while.

I dropped in at Trueman's gym in Newtown and caught the last of Bobby's sparring session. He had a massage and a shower and we went out onto King Street.

'Fancy a beer?' I said.

'Are you kidding? I'm strictly off it.'

'Why's that, champ?'

Bobby shot me a look. He wasn't dumb. He knew of my acquaintance with Bartlett. 'Oh, shit,' he said. 'You're going to tell me Teddy Simmonds is a bigger crook than Barry and not to listen to him.'

'Not a bit of it. You're not a child. You can talk to whoever you like. I just want to show you something. Where's your car?'

Bobby had a Beemer convertible he was proud of and happy to demonstrate. It was parked nearby and we walked there with him nodding graciously to people in the street who knew him.

'Pretty sharp, eh?'

'The car? Yeah.'

He laughed. 'Fuck you, Cliff. The sparring.'

I grunted. 'Not too shabby. Want you to meet an old mate of mine, Phil Sikes. Lives in Watsons Bay.'

Like all professional athletes, Bobby had trouble filling in the time when not training or performing. He was a family man but his wife, Jenny, handled that part of his life and

Bartlett's accountant dealt with the business side. He read a bit, mostly biographies of the well-known. He liked the movies and TV and did some work with the Aboriginal Youth Program but he didn't play golf. Time hung heavy and he was happy to go for a drive.

Phil Sikes was an ex-featherweight. A main event fighter in an unpopular division, whose career went nowhere. He won a lottery, retired and kept himself busy and amused by showing boxing films to sporting clubs and charity organisations. He had the best collection of boxing films in Australia and kept up to date via arrangements with US and European television providers and boxing managers and promoters.

Phil shook Bobby's hand enthusiastically. 'I've got a few of your fights. You had a great left hook.'

Bobby beamed. 'Still have.'

Phil nodded. 'Cliff here did pretty good as an amateur but didn't have the heart for the real game. He wanted me to show you something.'

We went into Phil's viewing room and he pulled down the blind to block the million-dollar view of the water and the boats. He had a huge TV and video set up and he handled a couple of remote-control devices like a chessmaster setting up the board.

Over the next two hours we watched films of the career of 'Sugar' Ray Leonard, then the undisputed welterweight champion of the world. Phil had somehow spliced together a sequence of films that ran from Leonard's defeat of Cuban KO artist Andrés Aldama to win the gold medal in the welterweight division at the 1976 Olympic Games through his early professional career, where he won a succession of fights, to his contests with Roberto Durán and his defeat of Tommy 'Hitman' Hearns.

Interspersed were extracts from documentaries on Leonard—his background, physical characteristics, training, tactics, techniques. No one said a word as we watched Leonard mature from a spindly cutie to a fighting machine. Leonard's reach was ten centimetres greater than his height and, as with Les Darcy, it let him do damage from a distance without extending himself and left him with abundant power when his opponent, tired of eating leather, was slowed down and easy to hit.

Phil and I had a couple of beers while watching the screen. Bobby refused at first but accepted during the Leonard/ Hearns fight.

'Moves well,' I said when the screen went blank.

'Never stops,' Phil said. 'No, he stopped against Durán and lost. Learned his lesson.'

'What about Hagler?' I said. 'Marvelous' Marvin Hagler was the world middleweight champion, a power-house puncher.

'One day,' Phil said. 'Be interesting.'

We thanked him and Bobby was quiet on the return drive, which he made cautiously. I'd left my car at the gym and he dropped me there.

'I get the point, Cliff. He'd kill me.'

'Possibly.'

'You see that left jab?'

I shook my head. 'Not really.'

'Exactly. Thanks, Cliff.'

3

Bobby Munday defended his Commonwealth title against an up-and-coming Maori fighter in Auckland and took a pretty heavy beating before rallying and knocking the Maori out in the tenth round. Then he retired.

Barry Bartlett bought me a drink when the retirement was announced and thanked me for helping Bobby see straight. Then I didn't hear anything from him for a long time. He stayed out of the courts and the papers and, with all my other concerns, I more or less forgot about him. So I was surprised when he phoned and asked to see me.

I was still in Darlinghurst then, although the gentrification wave that would move me out was building. Some of the streets had been blocked off to divert traffic and provide a quieter atmosphere and the building next to mine was being demolished, to be replaced by a block of up-market flats.

Like Bobby, Barry found it amusing to know a private eye and he'd dropped in a few times in the past to give me a ticket to a fight or just to talk boxing.

He turned up on time. His usual style was to pour scorn on any décor that wasn't brand spanking new—I had nothing that was—from car to clothes, but he was subdued as he lowered himself into my battered client chair.

He sat silently for a minute and I opened the bidding.

'How's Bobby doing? Haven't seen him for a while.'

He roused himself. 'Who?'

'Bobby Munday, the bloke we saved from brain damage.'

'Bobby, oh yeah. He's doing fine. Healthy financially and otherwise thanks to you and me.'

'How's he occupying himself?'

'He's the fitness coach of the fucking Sydney Swans. He reckons his son's a champion in the making. Poofter game if you ask me, but there it is.'

'So that's not why you're here.'

'No. Fact is, I'm very fucking confused.'

'Barry, I know you're ruthless and a bloody chancer, but I'd never have picked you as confused.'

Bartlett was a big man—over six feet and sixteen stone at least. He'd played rugby league and been a wrestler when young and some of the muscle had turned to fat. His colour was high, suggesting hypertension, and it rose as he half stood. 'You've got a fucking nerve talking to me like that. What're you? A two-bob keyhole-peeper. You . . .'

He slumped back into the chair, out of breath and out of anger. The hard lines of his craggy face sagged as if he'd lost a lot of weight lately. Jowls well on the way. His forehead under the receding hairline was damp and he mopped it with a handkerchief he pulled out of his pocket. His voice emerged on a breathy wheeze.

'Shit, I'm sorry, Cliff. I'm not meself.'

I had a bar fridge in the office. I opened it and took out some bottled water. I had a bottle of Black Douglas scotch in the deep bottom drawer of my desk and paper cups. I made a couple of mid-strength drinks and passed one across to Barry.

'Have you got medication for that blood pressure?'

'Yeah. And for everything else.' He took a long swallow and managed a short-winded laugh. 'Truth is the old ticker's not too hot. Waiting for the results of some more tests, but it doesn't look great. The quack says the best treatment is to avoid stress. How do I do that if I'm being conned?'

'Who by?'

He tossed off most of his drink. 'Fucking direct, aren't you?'

'Only way to go, mate. If you're going to be a client you have to stay alive long enough to tell me the problem and pay me a retainer. Unless you get a grip on yourself there's no time to lose.'

'You're right, you're right.' He put the paper cup with only an inch or so of fluid in it on the desk and pushed it away. A self-denying gesture of sorts. I took a solid belt of my drink.

Barry mopped his face again and leaned forward, lowered his voice. 'Here's the thing, mate. I was married—well over twenty-five years ago, now. It didn't work. I still rooted every woman I could get my hands on and my wife left me after a few years. There were two kiddies—a boy and a girl. I hardly knew their bloody names, I was so busy making a quid and staying alive.'

It was typical of people like Barry to flavour explanation with a touch of apology and a stronger touch of self-justification.

'Anyway,' he went on, 'she took the kids back to England—she was a Pom like me—and divorced me. She didn't ask for maintenance or anything and that was the last I heard of her . . . and them.'

'Until?' I said.

'Yeah, until this kid turns up claiming to be my son. His name's Ronald Saunders and he says he was adopted by Sylvie's—that's the wife's name—second husband and took his name.'

'Has he got any proof he's your son?'

'He's got a couple of photos of Sylvie holding a baby he says is him.'

'No birth certificate?'

'He left it back in the UK. He's applied for a copy, and the adoption papers.'

'What about a passport?'

'He's got that. British. So he must've had a birth certificate.'

'Nothing from his mother and stepfather?'

Barry shook his head. 'Both dead in a car accident. Showed me a newspaper clipping.'

'What about the sister?'

'Um, Barbara. He says she left home when she was sixteen and he thinks she's on the game in London. They're not in touch.'

'It's conveniently vague,' I said. 'What makes you think it's true?'

'Three things. He's the spitting fucking image of me when I was that age and he's got the same in-your-face attitude.'

I had a fair idea from his behaviour what the answer would be but I asked the question anyway. 'What's the third thing?'

He drew in a deep breath. 'I want to believe it. I've had a rackety life. I've got a lot of . . . competitors and no real friends. Haven't had a relationship with a woman for years. I've just used professionals and that's a fucking lonely life.' He looked embarrassed and fiddled with his cuffs. 'And . . . if I'm on the way out, I'd like to think there was someone to keep things going. Someone close.'

I nodded. 'What does this Ronald want?'

'Ronny? Nothing. He just wants to work for me, with me.'

'Learn the criminal trade, as it were?'

'I know you like taking the piss, Hardy.'

Hardy now, I thought. *What happened to Cliff and mate?*

'I'm a legitimate businessman these days, more or less. A developer, an entrepreneur, as they say. I could use someone

19

I could trust and hand things over to. Even if the heart stuff's fixable, I'm not getting any younger. And I make no bones about it: I'm a lonely man.'

'Okay.'

He looked around the room—at the windows, the crumpled venetians, the dented filing cabinet and at me.

'You're not doing so good,' he said. 'I'm offering you work and you're coming the high hat.'

'I said okay. Tell me what you want.'

'I want you to investigate him. Meet him, weigh him up, talk to him. Then see what he does, where he goes, who he meets.'

'What if he's not who he claims to be—or if he gets pissed off at being investigated?'

'I'll have to take that chance, but if you're as good as you're cracked up to be, he'll never know you're checking.'

Flattery now, I thought. Oscar Wilde said the flatterer is seldom interrupted, but Barry stopped right there and I had that sense I get with a lot of clients, probably most. There was something he hadn't told me.

'Ronny showed up a few months ago. I liked him. Couldn't help it. He's likeable. He needed money so I gave him a few little jobs to do and paid him. Nothing much.'

'Nothing much of a job, or nothing much of money?'

'Both. So he knows some of the things I do.'

'Like?'

'Shit, paying off politicians and officials to steer things my way. Everyone does it. It's still the only way to do business in this town.'

I shook my head. 'It's the quickest way maybe, or the easiest, but it's not the only way.'

He became aggressive again. 'Listen, this is something you wouldn't understand at your level. You borrow money to get things done. At interest from people who charge an arm and a leg and are fucking impatient. Every day you run over your date to pay back eats you alive. So you have to speed up development decisions, rezonings, environmental reports, permissions . . .'

I did understand it. I understood that it meant the money providers got heavy with the borrower and the borrower got heavy with the people he was buying. And other people got heavy with them. It wasn't a world I wanted to get into.

He read my mind. He leaned forward, picked up his drink and drained it. 'Like I said, I've got . . . competitors and there's things I don't want certain people to know. I'm worried that Ronny might be a plant.'

'Suppose he is, what then?'

'Nothing. I'm disappointed and I piss him off. That's all.'

'What if I find out he's a con artist and who put him up to it?'

He opened his hands. 'Then I know the score. I'm a winner and so are you, Cliff.'

4

I didn't have many qualms about working for someone like Barry Bartlett. As far as I knew he'd never killed anybody, and I'd worked for lawyers and politicians who'd stretched the laws to breaking point and beyond. Sometimes it was a hard line to draw. This sounded more or less like a personal problem, although Barry's mention of people he called his competitors (colour them enemies) sounded a warning note. But he was right about my financial situation; the windows needed cleaning and the venetians needed to be replaced.

I had him sign a vaguely worded contract and pay me a retainer. He gave me an address for Ronny Saunders and the registration number of the company car he was driving.

'Have you checked him out at all yourself?'

'Nah. Didn't have the energy. And there seemed to be plenty of time, then. Thought about it, but . . . Then I remembered you.'

23

I said I had a few things to clean up first before getting started.

'That's okay,' Barry said, giving me his card. 'BBE is having a drinks party at my offices the day after tomorrow. Ronny'll be there. You can kick off then. You'll see some familiar faces.'

'BBE?'

'Barry Bartlett Enterprises.'

'Of course.' I remembered occasionally seeing Barry's picture in the society pages of the magazines they kept at my doctor's surgery, but the name of his business hadn't really registered.

He tossed his cup at the waste-paper bin. It hit the rim and fell in. 'Till Friday. Have a shave,' he said. 'Bring a woman, if you like, and wear a fucking suit.'

I did have a couple of things on hand—finishing up on a dodgy car insurance claim and the vetting of a company's security system, which involved trying to beat it and could be fun—but I intended to spend some of the time checking on Barry Bartlett himself. The fortunes of people like him rise and fall and where he was in the cycle could have a bearing on the job he'd assigned me, and particularly on my chances of being paid.

I knew Barry had made money through the use of a stevedoring company and a number of corrupt customs officials in the past. If you could circumvent the payment of import duties and penalties on certain cargoes you could provide the market with cheap goods about which no questions would be asked. As far as I knew this operation hadn't involved drugs. I made some phone calls to check on the current state of play. I didn't trust that Barry had told me everything.

I spoke to a couple of wharfies in pubs and a 'retired' customs officer in a Darlinghurst bistro and learned that Barry, like this guy, had got out of that business just before a Royal Commission and a crackdown.

Jimmy Cook, a financial journalist, told me that BBE was a middle-to-heavyweight player in Sydney's ever-increasing development scene these days, making sensible bids for projects and so far delivering results on time.

'What about union problems, cash-flow hold-ups, that sort of thing?' I asked.

I could hear Cook expel smoke as he spoke. 'Clean bill of health. Let me know if you hear any different.'

'Bullshit!' Harry Tickener said the next day when I gave him Jimmy Cook's assessment of Barry Bartlett's current business status.

Harry was an old friend who'd worked for almost every newspaper ever published in Sydney and had been fired by most of them. He ran a newsletter called *Sentinel* with the logo 'We Name the Guilty Men'. He did, too, and he spent almost as much time fighting libel writs as collecting information and writing his exposés. *Sentinel* had some backing from a couple of radical unions and individuals, got some advertising from a left-wing community radio station and depended to a large extent on volunteer labour. I'd done some pro bono work for Harry myself.

Harry put his sneakered feet up on a desk of about the same vintage as mine and scratched at the fringe of ginger hair he retained. 'Barry Bartlett's got his finger in some very dirty pies but he wears thick gloves.'

'Good writing,' I said. 'Have you had a go at him?'

'No, he's got that shyster Todd Silverman in tow and I've just got clear of a slander action that would've finished me if it hadn't fallen over at the last minute. I don't need Silverman up my arse.'

At that time, Harry ran the operation out of a small terrace house in Macdonaldtown—two down, two up, no room to swing a cat anywhere. The room that served as his office had space for his chair, a desk, two filing cabinets and a stool. Otherwise every surface was covered with paper, every cranny was packed with books and files. I squatted on the stool with my knees lifted nearly to my waist. A couple of flies buzzed around looking for somewhere favourable to land.

'What sort of pies?'

Harry took a no-frills can of insect killer from a drawer in the desk and zapped the flies. Then he sneezed violently.

'Shit, I'm allergic to that stuff.'

I said, 'You need a low-allergy spray.'

'I need a lot of things I haven't got. Bartlett's development operation's legitimate enough as those things go, but it's partly a front.'

'For?'

Harry waved his hand at a pile of manila folders. 'I wish I could say I've got evidence like the stuff in there—statements, analyses, statistics—but I can't. There's something big, very big, behind what Bartlett does. You get hints from the names of people he employs, from the overseas trips he takes and the things he invests in.'

'Like?'

'Trucking companies, cruise ships, mineral exploration. Rumours of something to do with oil.'

'Profitable concerns, surely. Australian business on the move.'

'Yes, but with no discernible connection between them. In that kind of business it's an economic imperative that one hand shakes another. I'm certain there *is* a connection and it's a good bet that it's very dodgy. I'm not even sure Bartlett knows what's really going on himself.'

'That's vague. I can see why you haven't written anything.'

'Not yet. I'm thinking about it. So he's offered you a job, has he?'

'Come on, Harry. Not in the way you imply. I gave up working for other people long ago. He wants me to investigate something personal.'

'Are you going to do it?'

'I need the work.'

'If I weren't a friend of yours I'd ask you to keep your eyes and ears open for me but I won't. I know you'll play it straight for as long as you can.'

'That's not a vote of confidence.'

'You've got some sort of obligation to Bartlett, haven't you?'

'Not exactly. He did the right thing by someone he could've exploited. I respected that.'

'Hitler was good to his dogs. Just be careful, Cliff. Be very careful.'

'It's a personal thing,' I said, knowing that it might not be.

'Nothing's personal,' Harry said, 'not entirely.'

5

I had a contact at a clipping agency used by all sorts of people who wanted to know what the newspapers were saying about them and their clients, and how they were looking in photographs. I rang him and asked what he had on file for Barry Bartlett.

'Nothing juicy recently, just reports of developments and society-column stuff,' he said after doing a check.

'That'd please him. What about back a bit?'

'Quite a lot—dubious business stories, bit about managing boxers.'

'What about when he played football?'

'A few things. He didn't play first grade for very long.'

'Photos?'

'One, when he copped a suspension. He'd have been in his late twenties.'

'That'll do. Could you fax it? Usual arrangement?'

That meant a payment into his TAB betting account.

'It'll be rough, grainy.'

'That's Barry.'

I sat in the office and waited for the fax machine to kick into life. The sheet shuttled through and I saw that my guy hadn't exaggerated. Barry had been snapped opportunely rather than posed; physical surroundings and lighting were all against a clear photo. He was on the move, gesturing violently at someone, and his features were a bit contorted, but it was recognisably a younger, thinner Barry with the years and the indulgence stripped away. I studied it carefully before slipping it into the file I'd opened on the case.

Barry's invitation was for 6.30. It was that time of year when it could be hard to decide what to wear, but not this time—I only had one suit. A woman was harder; there was no one 'in my life', as they say. I decided to ignore that invitation. Who knew? There could be a single woman there looking for company.

The offices of BBE were in Alexandria in a sort of business park that had been created out of sold-off railways land. These were the days before Alexandria got tarted up and the look-alike buildings were laid out among concrete paths, white gravel sections and struggling, newly planted trees. The office blocks featured user-friendly ramps and lighting and there was a row of hopeful shops with chairs out front catering to the eating, drinking and smoking needs of the workers.

BBE occupied an entire two-storey building; not the biggest but not the smallest. I arrived at 7 pm with the light dimming and the building fighting back with a lot of discreetly placed fluorescent. There was a set of wide glass doors and I could see a congregation of well-dressed people immediately inside milling about with glasses in their hands. Waiters in white mess jackets and black pants circulated with drinks trays. It all looked welcoming, but entry wasn't just a matter of rocking up—you had to run the guest-list gauntlet.

The first face I saw was familiar—Des O'Malley, guarding the door, looking uncomfortable in his suit and a too-tight collar. He was burly, running to fat, and had a livid red birthmark on the left side of his face that had probably made him angry from the day he first became aware of it.

'Gidday, Des. Expecting me, I hope.'

'Yeah.'

'Looks like a nice party.'

'It was, till you got here. I'll kick the shit out of you one of these days, Hardy.'

'But not while we're working for the same guy, eh?'

'Give it time.'

O'Malley was an ex-middleweight boxer who, after throwing one fight too many and too obviously, had been avoided by managers and promoters. Then he'd worked as a standover man. He was a full-blown heavyweight now. I'd run up against him a few times in the past, always unpleasantly.

'Any time you like, Des, as long as it's just you and me. Somewhere without two of your mates in their steel-capped boots.'

O'Malley was better at physical than verbal sparring. He swore and would've spat if the tiles in front of him and the polished floor behind him hadn't been so pristine. He stepped aside and I went in.

Pot plants, chairs, table and a desk in the reception area had been pushed aside to provide a party space. Two long trestle tables held bottles, glasses and finger food. A microphone and a lectern had been set up at the end of the room under a banner that read: BBE CELEBRATES 10 YEARS OF DEVELOPMENT.

About a hundred besuited men and more than half that number of well-dressed and coiffured women were drinking champagne from flutes and nibbling canapés. I took a glass and drifted around. I was looking at a bunch of BBE brochures set out on a coffee table that had been pushed into a corner.

'Hello, Hardy.'

I turned to see a tall, white-haired man in a suit that would've cost three times as much as mine approaching me with a glass in one hand and a paper plate in the other. He put the plate, well-stacked with crackers anointed with cheese, anchovies and other things I couldn't identify, down on top of the brochures.

He put out his now free hand. 'Keith Mountjoy. Surely you remember me?'

I shook the soft, moist hand. 'Sir Keith.'

He nodded. 'For my sins.'

'Plenty of those.'

He released a well-fed, whisky-and-cigar-cured laugh. 'You haven't changed since that time you cost me a lot of money.'

With Des O'Malley and Sir Keith, my past was catching up with me. I'd been hired once by the Greyhound Racing Association to investigate claims of race fixing. It turned out that one of Sir Keith's trainers was involved and it had cost him money to minimise the penalty. He'd tried, but failed, to suppress the whole thing by offering me an inducement.

'You seem to have done pretty well since those days,' I said.

He popped a cracker into his mouth and chewed enthusiastically. 'Yes, yes, head's well above the waterline, thank you. What's your connection with good old Barry?'

'What's yours?'

'Oh, this and that. Hullo, here's the man himself.'

Barry, in a suit costing about the equivalent of Sir Keith's and draped in the same paunch-concealing style, was coming towards us.

His hands were empty, so he was able to clap both of us on our shoulders. 'Keith, Cliff, good to see you both. Having a good time?

'Sorry,' he went on, without waiting for an answer, 'I have to break this up. I've got someone I want you to meet, Cliff.'

'I'd better find the better half,' Mountjoy said. He cast a reluctant look at his abandoned plate and stumped away.

Barry pointed. 'She's the slant piece in the white.'

A tiny Asian woman, wearing a gleaming tight white dress, propped up on very high heels and with glossy black hair piled high to give her extra height, half turned towards the approaching Mountjoy and handed him her empty glass.

'She runs the show,' Barry said. 'Big mining money and getting bigger. Mining's the future of this wonderful country, Cliff. Rake up any money you can and get into it.'

'Are you into it?'

Barry didn't answer. He shepherded me through the crowd, nodding and smiling as he went.

'No woman, mate?'

'Not tonight.'

'Might be a spare heifer you can cut out.'

Barry liked to make reference to his very brief spell as a jackeroo. He led me towards where a tallish, youngish man was standing listening to a couple of older men.

'Cliff,' Barry said, 'I'd like you to meet my long-lost son, Ronny Saunders, Bartlett that was. Ronny, this is an old mate of mine, Cliff Hardy.'

Bartlett/Saunders turned away from the seniors and put out his hand.

'Gidday, Mr Hardy.' His London accent made the greeting sound ironic.

Barry laughed. 'He's learning the language . . . trying to.'

I shook the hand at the end of a well-muscled arm coming off a well-muscled shoulder. 'Nice to meet you. Your dad still sounds like a Pom to me. What d'you think?'

Ronny grinned and Barry butted in before he could speak. 'They pick me as an Aussie at Heathrow.'

I nodded. 'As soon as you go through with your British passport.'

Barry just managed to conceal his annoyance. 'Loves a joke, does Cliff,' he said. 'I'll leave you to chat. I've got to get this thing underway.'

I finished my drink and Ronny reached for the glass. 'Let me get you another one.'

'You're not drinking?'

'I've had two already for my nerves. I'm not used to bubbly. Have to pace myself.'

Or be careful, I thought as he moved away towards the drink waiters. Barry's lifestyle and habits had turned him into a jowly, late-middle-aged—and possibly very ill—Everyman. There was no discernible resemblance between him and young Ronny now, but Ronny's likeness to the old photo I had of Barry was striking. The same broad, hard planes to the face, the same aggressive jaw and dark, probing eyes. The hair was different; Barry's was thinning even when he was young and Ronny had a full crop, but male baldness comes down the female gene stream.

He returned with my champagne and orange juice for himself. I thanked him and we looked to where Barry and two other men were conferring near the lectern and microphone.

'Dad said I didn't have to listen to this,' Ronny said. 'He reckons it's all pats on the back stuff between him and some of his investors.'

'Aren't you interested in the financial side of his business?'

'Yes, very, but I'm not privy to everything. What do you . . . ?' He moved towards the periphery of the crowd and I had no option but to follow him because he obviously wanted to ask a question.

We were over where the clutch of imported-for-the-event pot plants almost afforded us privacy. Party chatter had died down and Ronny kept his voice low. 'You don't look like a businessman, if you don't mind me saying. What's your connection with Dad?'

'You mean what do I do?'

He smiled, exhibiting the same sort of charm that Barry could still display when he was in the mood. 'I suppose I do. Sorry, it's just that I'm anxious to learn as much as I can about the business. I just wondered . . .'

'I'm a private detective. I'm keen on boxing and I took an interest in a fighter Barry was managing a while back. I did Barry a favour.'

'Oh, I see. That must be interesting work,' he said, but

he didn't sound very interested. I nodded; he said it'd been nice talking to me and he moved away, sipping his orange juice. I hadn't had much of a chance to ask him anything, but I'd at least checked him out, and I was thinking about leaving when I was aware of someone else joining me in the medium seclusion.

'Excuse me,' she said. Husky voice. 'Is that the son?'

She was tall and dark, wearing a stylish pants suit and holding a half-full glass. Her hair was drawn back into a tight bun and her far from ugly face was dominated by a pair of black-rimmed spectacles. I stopped thinking about leaving as I considered her question. But nothing about her manner suggested that it was worth trying to pick her up. I said that it was indeed the son.

'Thank you.'

She walked straight over and spoke to him, standing very close. He gave her the charming smile and their heads dipped together as they spoke. I shrugged and moved towards the door.

Des O'Malley sneered at me as I approached. I emptied my glass and handed it to him. He had no alternative but to take it and I mimed a left hook to his mid-section as he stood there holding the fragile glass gingerly in his meaty hands.

I was in my car and turning the ignition key before it struck me that I'd seen the dark woman in the glasses before. But where and when and who she was eluded me.

6

Barry had said he was taking Ronny up to Palm Beach for the rest of the weekend, so I spent some time bringing my notes up to date on the car insurance scam and thinking about trying to breach a security outfit's own security.

Zac Dawson's business was installing and servicing surveillance and monitoring equipment—listening devices, cameras, infra-red beams, sensors, that sort of thing. He was ex-army like me and we'd done jobs for each other over the years. We'd met in a pub up at the Cross a week or so earlier, when he'd said he had a proposition for me. He'd bought the first round, which is always a good start for a proposer.

'Have you heard of a mob called Botany Security Systems, Cliff?'

'No.'

'Newish and going to be big, I'd say. They provide bodyguards, nightwatchmen (and women), payroll protection and such. Bit of a muscle mob, I'm told, headed by this South African hard case.'

I nodded and drank some wine. Zac is a small, wiry, intense type who doesn't drink. He's a qualified electrician and sound engineer and a hands-on type who says he can't afford to be one per cent off at any time. I've seen him crawl into spaces you wouldn't fit a cat.

'They operate out of an office complex in Bunnerong Road, Little Bay. The weird thing is, the premises themselves have bugger-all security. Just a shitty fence you could push over and a gimcrack guard booth for checking the employees' passes.'

'Sounds like they need your services.'

'They do and I've convinced the guy who's second in charge to hire me but the top guy isn't interested. Believes in manpower.'

Zac said this scornfully and drank his mineral water.

'Whereas you,' I said, 'believe in . . . ?'

'Science. I've got to convince the boss man that he needs a complete upgrade.'

'How?'

'Breach what he's got.'

'You're the expert.'

'It's a two-man job. I've been in there already. I need someone who hasn't.'

Zac sketched out a plan. It sounded pretty wild and I told him I'd think about it.

I had been thinking about it, and Zac'd been pestering me. He was offering good money and in the end it was too hard to resist and I gave in.

So on Sunday night I sat in the Longboard wine bar in Bronte waiting for Bruce Talbot, the mark. When he came in, swaggering, an overweight man in his early thirties in a flash suit and with carefully arranged, thinning, dirty blond hair, he was immediately recognisable from Zac's description. He was already drunk, as Zac had said he'd be, and looking for trouble.

'He's got problems,' Zac had said. 'I kept a watch on the vulnerables for a while. This dickhead plays tough but isn't and he won't learn.'

Talbot proceeded to drink a lot, talk loudly and make passes at several women. Eventually he overstepped the line and a man several kilos lighter took him outside and left him hunched over and vomiting. I intervened before more damage was done, cleaned him up and drove him home. He insisted I come in for a drink, then he passed out.

I located his security pass to the Botany Security Systems complex, photographed and measured it and left.

Barry rang me on Monday morning. 'You didn't stay long at the party. Looked around and you were gone.'

'Not my scene.'

'What did you think of Ronny?'

'He seemed a nice enough kid, respectful but not a softie.'

'You know what I mean.'

'The physical resemblance is strong but how many convincing Anastasias turned up?'

'Who?'

'Never mind. You seem to have made up your mind and he's happy to call you Dad. I wonder what he called his stepfather.'

'You're sceptical.'

'So are you. Look, Barry, the thing that concerns me is the inability to do much checking on his story. I can get a copy of the birth certificate, but so can anyone. It doesn't prove it's him. Unless you want me to fly to England and talk to the people in Coronation Street.'

'No, no, I'm not that doubtful. It's just that certain things are in the balance right now and if some bastard did have the idea of planting someone close to me . . .'

'Is there anyone who'd go to that amount of trouble?'

'Who knows? It's a dog-eat-dog world out here.'

'This kind of stress isn't good for your hypertension. Or anything else.'

'I know, that's why it'd be good to have someone . . . Look, what I want you to do is just keep tabs on him,' he repeated. 'See where he goes, who he sees.'

'Isn't he with you most of the time?'

'No. I send him out on jobs. Have him look at construction sites, meet people. He's young; he doesn't want to hang out with an old fart like me.'

'You said you're paying him?'

'Yeah, a bit.'

'How much is a bit?'

'Fuck you.'

'Why I ask is, if he seems to be spending a lot of money over and above what you give him, then questions arise.'

He saw the point. 'A couple of hundred a week and he's got a company car, as I said.'

'He can't meet the rent on a Paddo flat with that sort of money.'

'It's one of my places. I'm letting him use it.'

'Credit card?'

'Just for the petrol.'

'Keep it like that.'

'Okay. Shit, I hate this.'

'You can drop it if you like.'

'No. I've got to be sure.'

'Are you still handling fighters?'

'A couple, more or less at arm's length through Sally Brewer.'

That was a surprise. Sally Brewer was a forty-plus hard case who'd taken over a boxing gym from her father, Rex, a legend of the business. She trained and managed boxers and had a few fighting around Australia and the

Pacific and was doing okay. I'd known Rex well, knew Sally slightly.

I told Barry to give Ronny the afternoon off but ask him to drop in on Sally's evening session around 6 pm so he could acquaint himself with that area of Barry's interests. I said I'd pick him up as he left BBE, see how he spent the free time and meet up with him at Sally's gym.

'Why there?' Barry said.

'I miss the smell of the sweat and the resin, don't you?'

He didn't reply and hung up.

Ronny's blue Holden ute roared up out of the underground car park of the BBE building and headed towards the city. He stopped at the first public phone he spotted and made a call. Then he drove to Surry Hills and parked illegally in Riley Street. If he stayed there too long BBE would be up for a fine.

I stopped, obstructing traffic, and watched him walk into a Lebanese restaurant. I got moving and found a semi-legitimate parking spot. If it wasn't, that'd be another expense for BBE. I walked back on the other side of the street. Ronny had taken his place at one of the pavement tables under an umbrella. The day was cool and windy with clouds that could mean anything. An umbrella might be the go.

Traffic in the street was heavy and my view of Ronny was blocked from time to time. He seemed relaxed, lit a cigarette and studied the menu. A waiter approached and he ordered something that turned out to be a beer. He smoked and drank and then, suddenly, the cigarette was gone and he was on his feet—the perfect gentleman. The woman I'd seen on Friday night, this time in oversized sunglasses despite the gloom, strode up and they were hugging and kissing.

Fast work, I thought.

She was dressed in a skirt and jacket rather than pants today, although with the same smart, tailored look. They settled into their seats and it was smiles and laughs and touches of the hands and menu-inspection and everything that goes with lunchtime-for-lovers.

Watching a couple enjoying themselves while completely unaware that their privacy is being violated isn't the most salubrious part of the job. Nor is taking a photograph of them. I had a mini-camera with a zoom function and got two good shots in between the passing traffic. I didn't like doing it. It reminded me of the old 'Brownie and bedsheets' days before the blessed advent of Lionel Murphy's no-fault divorce legislation.

I waited until they were served their meals and then went back to my car and drove around until I found a place where I could pick Ronny up again when he left. It took a while. I ended up further along the street on the same side and watched in the passenger-side mirror as they finished their coffee.

The woman stayed seated while Ronny went into the restaurant to pay. She took her sunglasses off to rub her eyes and the quick look I got of her face confirmed that I knew her from somewhere, but still didn't give me a name, time or place.

They walked, staying close together, to Ronny's ute. He unlocked the passenger door and ushered her in, then took off more sedately than he had previously and headed towards Paddington. I had the address of his flat and followed without bothering to stay close behind. The small block of flats had parking for tenants and Ronny took his slot. It was an ugly, liver-brick 1930s structure that would house only three or four flats. No security set-up. Ronny unlocked the door to the building. To do that he had to let go of her hand, but he kissed it first. Then they disappeared inside.

That was enough for me. I knew where he'd be in about four hours and had a pretty fair idea of what he'd be doing in the meantime. I found a pub and had lunch—a steak sandwich with salad, hold the chips, and a middy of light beer. I tried to remember how long it was since I'd been to the gym. Too long. I felt the flab at my waist. Not too bad but I pushed the toasted bread aside and promised myself a gym session the next day.

I was drinking the last of the beer, relishing it, with my mind turned off when it came to me where I'd first seen Ronny's bespectacled companion. Something about the way she moved and the way she wore her jacket and skirt, like a uniform, triggered the memory. She'd been present as a sort of adjunct at a ceremony I'd attended where my friend Frank Parker, then a detective inspector, had been awarded a medal for bravery he'd displayed at a nasty armed siege. Frank's coolness had resulted in saving a woman and two children from injury with minimum damage to the crazed gunman.

That had been four years earlier. The commissioner awarding Frank the medal had talked about the policewoman who'd been at the scene throughout. He'd mentioned her name, which I'd forgotten, but I remembered the way she'd gazed at Frank with open admiration. Shorter hair and no glasses but unmistakably the same woman. Here she was again, virtually in disguise with the severe hair arrangement and the specs. In civvies but still looking as if she was in uniform and still moving with a kind of drilled precision. It was London to a brick that she was now an undercover cop.

Plenty to think about and I had another drink to help the process. Frank was a superintendent with an inside track to higher rank these days, but still a friend, despite my low standing in the eyes of his colleagues. I wondered if he'd known the admiring female constable and how much he'd tell me about her if he did. Probably not much.

I drove back to Darlinghurst and parked where I had an arrangement with a non-driving house-owner who let me use his garage. I dropped the film in where I knew someone who would process anything from family snaps to bedroom frolics. I went up to the office, taking the stairs three at a time, and felt that my wind at the top of three flights was no better than fair. I phoned Frank, confident I'd catch him. The higher the rank, the more desk time. It irked Frank but he had a wife and a mortgage and he couldn't afford to stand still.

'Cliff,' he said. 'Good to hear from you.'

I could tell he meant it. When you've been sitting at a desk all day, a call from someone who's been out on surveillance and eating a counter lunch on expenses could seem like a breath of fresh air.

'How's life, Frank?'

'I wouldn't call it life, exactly. How're you, mate?'

'Okay. Working. Frank, d'you remember when you got that gong for putting the lid on the siege in Enfield?'

I could imagine him at his desk, in his suit, worried about what I might say next and fidgeting with things in front of him. Like me, Frank was an ex-smoker and sometimes needed to be busy with his hands to keep himself clear of the weed.

'Yes,' he said. 'You were there with that redhead . . . who was she again?'

'Doesn't matter,' I said. 'Do you remember a female constable who was there sort of getting a best supporting Oscar and looking at you as if you were Clint Eastwood without the widow's peak?'

Frank wasn't a vain man, or no vainer than most who can present respectably, but he'd notice open admiration when it came his way.

'I think I know who you mean, yes.'

'Do you have her name?'

'You know better than to ask me that by now. You think I'm going to give out the names of members of the police force?'

'She was just a cop on the scene, wasn't she? I might be able to pick it up from the media.'

'Why don't you do that?'

'Look, Frank, I'm not asking because I fancy her. If she's still on the force I reckon she's working undercover. If she's left the force it would put a whole other slant on things and make a difference to what I do next in this case I'm working on. It'd help to know.'

There was a silence while Frank digested this. A slow but very clear and clever thinker, he was annoyed that I'd overstepped the bounds of our friendship but I'd done that before and still kept his trust.

'I don't remember her name. I'll ask around a bit, more in her interest than in yours,' Frank said. 'I don't suppose you'd care to tell me who you're working for?'

'Client confidentiality.'

'Bullshit, there's no such thing in your game.'

'Personal code of honour, mate.' Then I thought it wouldn't matter if Frank knew who I was working for and what I was doing. Trust works both ways, and I didn't see there was any conflict of interest here. If this woman *was* an undercover cop it would add a whole other dimension to the case, and I didn't think Frank would be cooperative unless I told him a bit more.

'Okay. I've got a watching brief from Barry Bartlett. Nothing major, a personal matter.'

'Supping with the devil, Cliff. I hope you're using a long spoon.'

7

Brewer's Gym was at the back of a building in Erskineville Road near the railway bridge. Rex Brewer had trained some Australian and Empire (in those days) champions and a few world-ranked fighters. His boxers fought three times in Japan and the US for world titles but never quite cracked it. Weight problems, biased hometown referees and judges, loaded gloves—trainers and fighters always have excuses.

Boxing had been in the doldrums for years, waiting, as it has always done, for a new star to blaze in the firmament and re-excite the fickle public. Jeff Fenech had provided the crucial spark and suddenly tough young men were varying their football training with boxing workouts and some of them were opting for boxing as the quickest way to get what they wanted—which was cars, money and women, the order varying according to the individual. Sally Brewer, who'd had lean times after her father's death, was now benefiting from the Fenech-inspired revival. She had three Australian champions, two with world rankings, and a number of young boxers, promising and hungry.

I was late getting to the gym, delayed by the thick traffic in King Street as Newtown slowly shed its sleazy image and started its transition to metro chic. The Brewer gym was upstairs, the way a boxing gym should be, so a trainer can have a fighter run up and down a few flights fifty or so times. That peculiar smell these places have, a combination of sweat, liniment and cleaning fluids, drifted down to me as I climbed the stairs. In those days the aroma also included tobacco smoke.

I walked in through the open double doors to a cacophony of leather hitting leather, rubber soles shuffling on canvas, shouted instructions and explosive grunts. A train roared past, adding to the noise. It was all pretty much as I'd expected, with twenty or so men going through their routines and Sally, the one woman, up by the ring watching a sparring session.

'Hello, Sal,' I said. 'How's it going?'

She kept her eyes on the men in the ring after giving me the quickest of glances. 'Gidday, Cliff. Not bad, thanks.'

'Jeff Fenech's done you a favour, eh? The amateurs paying their fees and the pros making you a quid?'

She tapped the bell with a heavy ring on one of her fingers to end the round but she kept her eyes on the two fighters standing in their corners. She gestured to one of them to keep his guard up and circle left, away from a southpaw's lead.

'Wouldn't mind having this guy in the string,' she said, pointing at the other fighter.

They were both wearing headguards and it took me a few seconds and a closer look to see that the man she was referring to was Ronny Saunders. The shorts were too tight for him and the singlet too loose. There were crude tattoos on both forearms and he banged his gloves together in a way that indicated he'd done it many times before.

'Jesus,' I said.

Sally gave a harsh, cigarette-cultivated laugh. 'Know him, do you? Jesus?'

'No, but I know this guy.'

'Fuckin' Pom. Said he's Barry Bartlett's son. Barry's got a share in this place.'

'I thought it was yours.'

'It was. Then the bank had a piece and now Barry has. This Ronny said he wanted to look the place over and then he wanted to have a go. Hold on.'

She tapped the bell again and the fighters went into action. At a guess Ronny was a welterweight and his opponent was probably a middleweight. But Ronny was handling things easily, moving his opponent around and landing to the head and body.

'Look at him,' Sally crowed, 'knows how to fight a southpaw. He knows to get his front foot on the bloody outside and keep it there.'

'It's not easy to do,' I said.

'It is if you do it straight off, which is what he done. Confused Merv right from the start.'

I took another look at the man Ronny had manoeuvred into a corner and was peppering with punches. 'Is that Merv Martin?'

'Yeah, "Mighty" Merv. Don't look so mighty now, does he? I'd better stop this before he gets hurt.'

She pounded the bell a couple of times and the boxers dropped their hands. I noticed Ronny waited until he was sure Martin had moved first. They touched gloves. Martin was breathing heavily; Ronny seemed unstressed. He strolled across to where Sally stood and then appeared to notice me for the first time.

'Cliff,' he said and raised a glove. 'Dad said you used to be pretty good. How about it?'

'Not on your life,' I said. 'A few years ago, maybe, and I wouldn't have let you bamboozle me with that anti-southpaw stance.'

He leaned on the ropes. He had the sloping shoulders and the natural ease of movement of an athlete. 'Were you a left-hander?'

'When I wanted to be.'

It was true I was more or less ambidextrous at sports but right-handed at other things. It was also true that Merv Martin was no slouch. He'd been a contender for the national middleweight title and had beaten some well-regarded fighters. He was also nominally managed by Barry Bartlett, though Sally Brewer did the work.

'I'll get changed and we'll have a drink,' Ronny said. 'What brings you here, anyway?'

I put my arm around Sally and she stiffened. 'We're old mates. Well, I knew her dad.'

Ronny nodded, holding out his hands for one of Sally's minions to unlace his gloves. 'Was he any good, Sal?'

Ronny was one of those people who remembered names and used them easily on first acquaintance. Sally hip-bumped me away. 'My dad said so. Or was it my grandad? Ancient history. I reckon he was probably better at the blarney than the biff.'

'So Barry's got you keeping an eye on me?'

We were in the bar of the Bank Hotel with beers and a saucer of peanuts. Ronny was wearing an Arsenal cap and a scarf in the club colours.

'What makes you think that?' I said. 'And what happened to "Dad"?'

'Come on. You're like a fish out of water at that poncy drinks party and then you happen to show up at the gym. You're a private eye with some sort of connection to Barry. That's how I prefer to think of him when he's setting a dog on me. I'm not bloody stupid.'

I drank some beer. 'No, you're not, and you can handle yourself in the ring. Where'd you pick that up?'

'Where d'you reckon?'

'Army maybe, but then there's the prison tats.'

He laughed. 'Got it in one. Both places. I spent more time in detention than on the bloody parade ground.'

'Did you tell Barry that? And don't call me a dog.'

The aggression vanished as quickly as it had come. 'Sorry, no offence. I was upset that he didn't trust me. I am his son, you know.'

'I think I believe you. Be handy if there was a bit of solid evidence.'

He took a handful of peanuts, munched them and washed them down with a gulp of beer. 'There could be. My sister. Maybe I could get in touch with her. Maybe she could even come over here.'

That's what it'd take, I thought, *until we link up telephones with television.* 'Do you have her address?'

'Not exactly, but I might be able to track her down.'

I remembered Barry telling me the sister's profession. Plenty of work in that line in Sydney, but it all sounded iffy and I must have looked sceptical.

'Have you ever had to prove who you were, Cliff?'

'Often.'

'No, I mean . . .'

'I know what you mean. It's difficult. The sister might be a help. Would she have her birth certificate? Did your stepfather adopt her as well?'

'No. I dunno why. She was a bit older, she goes by Bartlett, or she did. God knows what . . .'

'It's all right. Barry told me about her.'

He took a defiant gulp of his beer. 'I'm not ashamed of her. Looking back, I reckon Len could've been fiddling with her. I didn't do much better than her, when all's said and done. I missed prison for assault and battery by a whisker. Did a small stretch for possession. That's between you and me.'

He was almost recruiting me. I knew it and somehow didn't resent it. Maybe I'd been more impressed by the way he'd handled Mighty Merv than I should have been. I was most of the way to believing he was who he claimed to be, but still very uncertain about why he'd turned up now and what his agenda was. And I was factoring in the tall brunette with the long stride and the glasses.

'Are you going to put in a report on me to Dad... Barry?'

'I have to, eventually. It'd be good to know a few things first. Like why have you turned up just now?'

'I always meant to come over, but never got around to it. Didn't have the money. That's all.' His voice was raised by then, as if he was answering an unspoken accusation.

Our glasses and the saucer of peanuts were empty. It was just me and him in a Newtown pub at eight o'clock on a Monday night with a light rain falling outside and the headlights shimmering through the raindrops.

'What'll your report say?'

'I haven't decided.'

He got to his feet with those easy, fluid movements. 'I'm going to see him. I'm going to tell him how we talked and . . .' He was almost shouting by now.

'Are you going to tell him how you handled Merv Martin? He's one of Barry's boys.'

'Is he?' he asked more quietly. 'He needs to learn how to keep that southpaw advantage. I'll tell Barry I might be able to get in touch with Barbara to convince him. I'll tell him it was your suggestion. That won't make you seem so bad.'

I got up. A few people looked around at us. I hadn't realised our conversation had seemed to turn into a confrontation.

'Be careful, Ronny,' I said. 'Barry's got a hell of a temper when things go against him. I don't know if you've spotted it but he's under a lot of strain. And his blood pressure . . .'

He nodded and walked out.

8

I was in the office mid-morning when the phone rang. I let the answering machine pick up the call.

'Cliff, this is Barry Bartlett. What the fuck are you doing? Ronny's disappeared and I—'

I snatched up the phone. 'I'm here. What do you mean disappeared?'

'What I say. He didn't show up at the office this morning and I've rung his flat ten times and he's not there.'

'Maybe he's having a haircut, finishing off something from yesterday.'

'No. He came to see me last night after he'd seen you. He accused me of spying on him, not trusting him . . . We had a row, a big one, and we both said things we shouldn't have.'

'Like?'

'Shit, I said his mother was a slag and his sister was a slut.

He said I abandoned them and let their mother fall into the hands of a fuckin' paedophile and . . .'

'Okay, I get the picture. We have to talk. Have you got a key to his flat?'

'Of course I have.'

'Meet me there as quick as you can and we'll have a look and ask about. I wouldn't worry too much. He's been around, Barry; he can handle himself.'

'I don't know. There's people . . .'

'What people? As I said, we have to talk—you can't go on being so fucking vague, Barry. I'll see you in Paddington.'

I got there first. Barry rolled up in a white Mercedes and came storming towards me as I got out of my car.

'You couldn't have been all that fucking subtle last night,' he said. 'He knew what you were doing.'

'Take it easy. We were on pretty good terms when he left me, not like you. Let's see how things look.' I pointed to the vacant car bay. 'His car's gone.'

'A detective genius.' Barry dug in the pocket of his rumpled suit jacket and produced a keyring. He selected a large key and marched up to the main door with it held out in front of him like a knight with a lance. But he couldn't get it in the keyhole. His hand was shaking. I took the key and unlocked the door.

'Which flat, Barry?'

'Number three, one flight up.'

'How many of these flats do you own?'

'I own the whole fucking lot.'

We went up a short flight of stairs to a landing that was only dimly lit by a small window. Barry stabbed at a light switch and swore when no light came on.

'Landlord responsibility,' I said.

'You'd make wisecracks at your mother's deathbed.'

'I did. She laughed.'

He'd pulled himself together and this time he got the door open without any trouble. We went into a short passage leading to a central sitting room with three half-open doors leading off it. Barry waved his hand.

An empty Great Western champagne bottle stood on the coffee table with two plastic glasses, one with a lipstick smear.

Barry looked at the bottle and the glasses and shrugged. 'Bedroom, kitchen and bathroom. All a bachelor needs. Two of the tenants are queers.'

There were four flats—two on the ground level and two above.

'What about the other tenant?'

'Hard to say. I'll have a look in the bedroom.'

I went to the bathroom. Did Ronny shave with a blade or an electric razor? Did he use prescription drugs? Did he wash his underwear in the bathroom basin? Detective work. Did a woman spend some time here? Lipstick smeared on the glass and on tissues in the waste bin said she did. A used condom dotted the i and crossed the t.

I joined Barry in the living room.

'Bedroom's a mess,' he said.

'He had a woman here, obviously.'

'I should bloody hope so. There's makeup on the pillow. Though you never know in this place . . .'

'I followed them here. Tall brunette he seemed to have met at your party.'

Barry shrugged. 'That's what parties are for sometimes.'

I went into the bedroom and kitchen, both messy. It was hard to decide when they were last used and by how many people. There were no clothes or shoes in the bedroom, no bags, but the soiled sheets hung half off the bed and two more dirty glasses lay abandoned on the floor, alongside a few used condoms. There were five coffee-stained mugs and a number of crumb-strewn plates in the kitchen. Ronny was better at footwork in the ring than at washing-up. Barry prowled around the living room; apart from the bottle and the glasses, it showed little sign of having been used.

'Nothing here,' he said.

'I wouldn't say that.'

He looked enquiringly at me.

'No sign of violence, no struggle. When we spoke on the phone you made some remarks about people. You were saying . . . ?'

'Nothing. Let's get out of here.'

We went out onto the dark landing. Barry slammed the door shut and tried the light again without success. He knocked on the door of the adjacent flat and got no response.

'You say you saw him with a woman?'

'She homed in—targeted him, it appeared to me.'

Barry was on the second step down. He swung around to look at me and lost his balance. I reached for him but he fell, bouncing off the wall, feet scrabbling uselessly at the stairs and hitting the bottom with a hundred-kilogram thud. I scooted down after him and found him lying flat on his back, one leg cocked under him. His lips were white and he was breathing in short, shallow gasps.

The door to the closest flat opened and a man in a silk dressing gown stood there, posed in the half-light like the ghost of Noël Coward.

'*What* is going on here?'

'Call an ambulance,' I shouted. 'I think he's had a heart attack.'

The man from flat one came back dressed in a white tracksuit and white sneakers. He had a pillow and I put it under Barry's head.

'Ambos are on the way.'

'Thanks,' I said. 'This is your landlord, did you know?'

'He still deserves help.'

I looked at him.

Barry's breath was still coming in short gasps and his eyes flickered open and then closed as if he didn't like what he saw. His colour was bad, greyish, and his mouth had an odd twist to it. Could you have a heart attack and a stroke at the same time? I didn't know.

The ambulance arrived and the paramedics made a quick examination.

'Stroke, I'd say,' one muttered as he helped his mate load Barry onto a stretcher.

Another tenant and his companion had appeared and someone who'd come to make a delivery was hanging around, making five of us.

'Who's going in with him?' the paramedic asked.

'Me,' I said.

They carried the stretcher out to where the ambulance stood and ran it into the attachments. Everyone followed. 'You a relation?' the paramedic said as he locked the stretcher down.

'No, a friend.'

'Ride in there with him. Keep him awake if you can.'

I nodded thanks to the helpful tenant and climbed into the ambulance, which took off at speed. I sat on a hard seat close to the stretcher while the other paramedic monitored Barry's blood pressure and other vital signs.

'How's he doing?' I said.

The paramedic shook his head and didn't answer. Barry twitched and muttered and then seemed to calm down. He tried to lift his right arm but couldn't. He curled the fingers.

'He wants to say something to you,' the paramedic said.

I bent my head down close to where Barry's lips, flecked with saliva, were moving.

'Find my boy,' he whispered.

part two

9

Barry was taken straight to Intensive Care at St Vincent's. I gave the hospital what details I could, which wasn't a lot; I could only guess at Barry's age. I knew his address but not the name of his doctor. I knew he was on some kind of medication for his high blood pressure but didn't know what.

'I'll ring his company and see what else I can find out.'

The admissions clerk pushed the phone and the directory towards me. I looked up BBE and rang, asking to speak urgently to someone in Personnel about the CEO.

A familiar voice came on the line. 'Hardy, what the hell's going on?'

'Who's this?'

'It's Keith Mountjoy. What . . . ?'

'How come you're there?'

'I'm Barry's partner. When he didn't show up for an important meeting this morning they called me in.'

I explained what had happened.

'Is he alive?'

'Only just, I think.'

'Personnel'll have those details. I'll get someone to phone them through to the hospital. Stay where you are and I'll meet you there and you can tell me what the hell you and Barry have been up to.'

'And you can find out how he's doing, too.'

'You'll be a smartarse once too often,' he said and hung up.

I sat in the standard kind of hospital waiting room with the old magazines, the anxious people and the annoying daytime TV. After half an hour Keith Mountjoy appeared at the door accompanied by a white-coat-clad doctor and beckoned to me. He must have made some calls before he arrived at another entrance. A knighthood carried weight and Sir Keith had Dr de Sousa, who he introduced, well under control. We went down the corridor to the room the doctor shared with two others, not then present.

Mountjoy was all authority. 'I want you to hear this, Hardy. Go on, Doctor.'

De Sousa consulted sheets on his clipboard. 'Mr Bartlett has suffered a seizure . . . a series of seizures.'

Mountjoy's voice dropped in volume the way voices do when death is in the air. 'What're his chances, Doctor?'

It was de Sousa's turn to shrug, having apparently regained some of his doctoral authority in the face of Mountjoy's uncertainty. 'Without knowing the cause, treatment is very difficult. All his signs are weak. In normal circumstances my advice would be to alert family members. You'll have to excuse me. I have other patients to attend to.'

Mountjoy slumped into a chair behind one of the low tables. I leaned against the wall while he took out his cigar case and a big gas lighter.

'The sprinklers might come on if you ignite that,' I said.

He put the case and lighter away. 'You're a smartarse.'

'You said that before.'

'Where's Ronald?'

'I told you. He's missing. Does it matter to you?'

'Bloody oath it does. Barry told me he was changing his will. Ronald's going to inherit Barry's share of BBE. Fifty-one bloody percent.'

'And yours is?'

He took the cigar from his pocket and fiddled with it. 'Less.'

'When did Barry tell you this?'

'A week ago, maybe ten days. Plenty of time for him to have actually done it.'

'Lucky Ronny, if he did.'

Mountjoy's grunt was noncommittal. 'And now you tell me the kid's missing. Why?'

'All I know is that Barry said they had a knock-down, drag-out row last night.'

'About what?'

'About me, partly.'

I couldn't see any harm in telling him why Barry had engaged me and how things had worked out, although I gave him an edited version. He listened without interrupting. When I'd finished he heaved his bulk up out of the chair.

'Let's go somewhere I can smoke. Can't think without smoking.'

'Must've been tough at the investiture. Those things take a while, I understand.'

He snorted as we walked to the designated smoking area near a lift, where a pot plant struggled in a mulch of butts. 'Why you haven't been dumped in the harbour years ago I'll never understand.'

Mountjoy lit his cigar and puffed luxuriantly.

'What do you think's happened to the kid?'

I was reminded of Barry's remark about 'some people'. 'Happened? Why should anything happen?'

'Who else would know about the changed will?'

'Search me,' I said. 'He told you, could've told a few people. He didn't tell me.'

'Did he tell you anything about the . . . current business climate?'

'No. Just that it was volatile, whatever that means.'

He inhaled the cigar smoke deeply and released it in little puffs as he spoke. 'Yes, it's very volatile. BBE can't be without direction. There'll have to be a meeting to set things straight. Ronald'll have to be consulted at least.'

'Only if Barry dies and if his will's been changed.'

'That's right, but at the very least he's going to be laid up for a while and it'd be good for him to see his boy and know that things are all right, wouldn't you think?'

I nodded. 'If you say so. I don't know anything about the paternal impulse.'

His deep draws had reduced the cigar considerably. 'I'll take care of the administrative side of things and make sure Barry's getting the best. Might have to move him to a private place. Now, you were on the job for how long?'

'Not long.'

'Found out a few things about Ronald?'

'I found out he's a very accomplished boxer.'

'Really? Afraid I don't see the relevance of that. Look, I'll issue a press release on Barry and it'll make the papers and maybe even the radio and TV news. That should send Ronald running back from wherever he's gone.'

'You'd think so.'

'But if it doesn't, for whatever reason, would you undertake to look for him?'

Sir Keith Mountjoy wasn't a man to like and he certainly wasn't a man to trust.

'Let's wait and see,' I said.

The news went out in brief reports on afternoon radio and the evening news on TV. No details, just a report that Barry was in Intensive Care and that his condition was of concern to his family and friends.

Mountjoy rang me early the following morning.

'Nothing,' he said.

'That's a worry.'

'And Barry's showing no signs of improvement as far as I can work out—still in Intensive Care, anyway. I tried to ask for more information and got nowhere. Apparently they'll only talk to next of kin and other medical people.'

'Who's Barry's doctor?'

'Apparently he's got a mob of them. I didn't know he had so much wrong with him. His GP and his heart specialist are in Randwick: Doctor Simon Abrahams and *Mister* Paul Templeton. They're in the same building, a medical centre across from the Prince of Wales. I don't think they'd talk to you or me either. I hate doctors—never go near them.'

You should, I thought, *from the look of you.*

'Is that right,' he said, 'that you can't post someone as missing for forty-eight hours?'

'More or less. It's flexible.'

'I don't want to do that unless it's absolutely necessary. By now, from what you said about seeing him boxing, you must know Ronald better than anyone else. I want you to look for him. I'll pay you.'

'I've still got some of Barry's retainer to work through. Are you willing to let the chips fall where they will?'

'What d'you mean?' The words came out slightly choked, as if smoke had got in their way.

'I think you know what I mean.'

'Do it, and stay in touch.'

He rattled off three numbers—for his office, his home and his car. Sir Keith was a worried man.

I caught a taxi back to Paddington and my car. I'd been too tired the night before to do anything but climb into a cab. I made a mental note to call someone at BBE to reclaim Barry's Merc. Then I went to my office and hit the telephone. My first call was to Sally Brewer. In the movies, Ronny would have turned up at the gym with his overnight bag and announced his intention of taking up a boxing career. Then he'd go on to win . . . But Sally hadn't seen him.

The next call was to my doctor, Ian Sangster. Ian is president of some doctors' organisation and well respected in the profession. I asked if he could clear the way for me to make contact with medicos Templeton and Abrahams. I needed to know what Barry's chances were.

Then I called Frank Parker.

'I thought I'd be hearing from you when I heard about Barry Bartlett,' he said.

'Yeah, well the boy's missing and hasn't been in touch even when the news on Barry went out. People are worried.'

'So instead of watching him you're looking for him?'

'Right, and I've seen him in the company of the police-woman we spoke about.'

'*You* spoke about. I didn't say anything about her.'

'Fair enough, but you said you'd ask around. There's something going on with Barry's business. I don't know what it is but people are jumpy, especially if Barry croaks, because the son comes into the picture then.'

'What people?'

'Sir Keith Mountjoy, for one.'

'Jesus Christ, talk about corruption. You've got yourself in the shit here, Cliff.'

'I get that feeling. But the kid's okay, I think, and I need to know what side your admirer . . . sorry, that woman is on. What was the date of that siege?'

He sighed and gave it to me. 'All I can tell you,' he said, 'is that she's still a member of the police service.'

'So she's undercover?'

'No comment, sorry.'

'That's okay. I'm going to have to tackle this another way.'

'I know. Be careful, Cliff.'

I collected the prints of the photographs I'd taken of Ronny and the woman at the restaurant and went by bus to the State Library where they had the *Sydney Morning Herald* on microfilm. I compared the photo I had with the one in the paper showing the uniformed policewoman in consultation with plain-clothed Frank. The photographer had got a good clear shot in favourable light. There was no doubt. With her hair concealed by her cap, her strong, high cheekbones and thin-lipped mouth were unmistakable. Senior Constable Bronwen Marr, who'd be going by another name now that she was undercover.

I sat outside the library and tried to replay the scene at the restaurant in my head. Ronny had arrived first and he'd looked a bit uncertain about where to put himself. Bronwen, or whoever she was now, had marched up confidently, familiar with the place. When Ronny had gone inside to pay she'd chatted with a bald-headed waiter.

I took a cab to Riley Street and arrived at the Bistro Beirut in time for a late lunch. I ordered felafel and dips and a chicken kebab with chilli sauce and rice. They served wine by the glass, so why not? A healthy glass of the house white. The bald waiter was there but not serving me. I ate quickly and as the other customers drifted away back to work I ordered coffee from Baldy. He looked irritated to be interrupted in his clearing away of plates and glasses. The restaurant closed for a couple of hours in the afternoon. When he delivered the coffee I thanked him and gave him a twenty-dollar note.

'I want to have a word with you,' I said, 'for fifty more.'

Waiters at places like that work for tips. He nodded and got back to his clearing up. I finished my coffee, paid the bill and left, taking the waiting spot I'd used before across the street. After twenty minutes he joined me.

'Are you the police?' he said.

I was wearing jeans, an open-necked blue shirt and a leather jacket. 'Sort of,' I said. 'Do I look like the police?'

'Sort of.'

I jerked my head to the left and we strolled along to where there was a postage-stamp sized park with a couple of seats. He lit a cigarette as we walked. We sat down and the first thing I showed him was a fifty; the next was my photo of Ronny and his friend.

'You know this woman?'

'I might.'

I gave him the fifty.

'What's her name?'

'Tania, I think.'

'You *think*?'

'Tania.'

'Other name?'

'Don't know.' He dropped his cigarette butt to the ground where it joined a lot of others. He stood on the butt, then felt in his pocket for his packet and I stopped him.

'Does she come here regularly?'

He was a small man, weak-chinned and nervous as well as bald. I was bullying him the way I guessed a lot of people had bullied him in the past and would in the future.

'Yes,' he said, 'regularly.'

'She wasn't there today. What does regularly mean?'

He sucked in a breath, avoided the pressure of my arm and got his cigarettes from his pocket. I didn't stop him. He lit up and blew the smoke away. The action seemed to lend him confidence.

'She's a nice woman,' he said.

'Is she?'

'Yes, and I don't think you're a nice man.'

'There's worse,' I said, 'and she could be in danger from them. I'm not interested in her except to find the young man she was with the other day. I'm what you might call their protector.'

'What was your question?'

I took out another twenty and added a five. Precise amounts sometimes have a telling effect.

'When will she be there next?'

After a pause he took the money. 'Tomorrow.'

'I'll be there, too. I'll just talk to her. You can trust me.'

He got up, blowing smoke. 'I'm from Lebanon, Mister Whoever-you-are, via several refugee camps. I don't trust anyone.'

10

The set of keys Barry had used to get into the building and Ronny's flat had fallen free when he'd hit the ground and I'd picked them up and put them in my pocket as a reflex action. With time on my hands and needing the exercise, I walked back to the office, collected my car and drove to Paddington. The Mercedes was still there under a paperbark tree, accumulating leaves and dust and grime. I'd alerted BBE but they hadn't picked it up yet, maybe had trouble finding a key.

I used Barry's keys and let myself into the flat. There was no sign that anyone had been there since our visit. I did a thorough search of the kitchen, living room and bathroom, examining things in the waste bins, delving into the upholstery of the chairs and couch, checking all drawers, all cupboards, all jars, the fridge, the freezer, the oven. I riffled through the couple of magazines lying about—the *Bulletin*, *Sports Illustrated*. Nothing.

That left the bedroom, where secrets are often kept and revealed. The bedside chests and the wardrobe yielded nothing. The bed base sat flat on the floor, saving me from having to crawl under the bed, and there was no headboard. I stripped the bed linen—sheets, one blanket—and removed the pillowslips. I shook out the sheets and an earring dropped to the floor. It was a gold clip-on with a small, dangling star. Not much, but something.

Back to the phone. I called BBE and told someone again about Barry's car. I phoned Dr Abrahams' rooms, choosing him because in my experience specialists are harder to get hold of and tougher to deal with than GPs, and was put through to him after a long wait.

'Mr Hardy,' he said in a sandpaper voice, 'that ratbag Sangster said you'd be in touch about Barry.'

'He is a ratbag, but a terrific bloke as well. Thanks for taking the call. Have you seen Barry?'

'No point. He's in a coma but I've spoken to the doctors there. He's in a very bad way.'

'Have they got the pathology report?'

'A preliminary. Inconclusive.'

'What medications was he on?'

'A bloody battery of them—for blood pressure, type 2 diabetes, arrhythmia, thyroid ...'

'So he could've dropped from any one of those causes?'

'Yeah. What, precisely, is your interest, Mr Hardy?'

I explained it to him, with no more details than he needed to know. He didn't say anything and for a moment I thought the line had gone dead.

'Doctor? Still there? I want to know what his chances are. It matters in what I'm doing.'

'I'm here,' he said. 'I think we'd better meet. I don't want to talk about this on the phone.'

'I don't understand.'

'You will. Can you be here this evening, say around seven o'clock?'

'Yes. I have to ring Mister Templeton and—'

His laugh was like a rasp on hardwood. 'Don't bother. He's on the other side in medical politics. Won't give you the time of day. I'm surprised Ian . . . no I'm not, he'd have enjoyed the thought of you having a go at him.'

'You're sure you can't tell me now what you know?'

'Oh, I suppose I could, but I want to get a look at you first.'

I was parked half a mile down the street from the Prince of Wales Hospital at 6.30, hoping to get a bit closer as the staff went off shift and the visitors went home. Didn't happen and I walked. Dr Abrahams was obviously an admirer of Ian Sangster and I guessed that, unlike many highly qualified professionals, he put no store in a person's wardrobe. Sangster, like me, was averse to neckties. I was still in the clothes I'd worn all day and my heavy beard was breaking through this late in the day.

Quite a few lights were still on in the medical centre and I went up the well-lit stairs to the second floor and along to Dr Abrahams' rooms. The reception area stood open. I went in and rapped on the counter. The door to the inner sanctum opened and a man came bustling out. He was below medium height, dressed in a dark shirt and trousers. No tie, no white coat.

'Mr Hardy?' An abrasive voice, but welcoming.

'Yes.'

We shook hands. His was hard and dry. He had a full head of wiry dark hair, a roundish face and a bristling moustache.

'Come in, come in,' he said, 'Cliff, isn't it? I'm Simon— Cy to my friends and enemies. Sit down, sit down.'

I sat in a comfortable chair in a comfortable room and before I could say anything he was talking again.

'Bloody Barry,' he said. 'I always thought I'd be talking to the cops one day or treating the poor bastard in a prison hospital. Well, it's not quite that. I expect you want me to get to the point.'

I expect you will, I thought. I nodded. That seemed to be enough response for him. He'd been searching through a filing cabinet while he was talking. He pulled out a file, slipped into his chair behind a cluttered desk and started leafing through it as though I wasn't there.

It gave me time to look around the room. There were a number of framed documents on the walls—degrees and memberships of professional bodies, awards received. The guy had the tickets.

He slammed the file shut. 'How long have you known Barry?'

'About ten years, maybe twelve.'

'What's the connection?'

Unusually for me, I didn't resent being interrogated. There was something direct and forthright about him that inspired respect.

'Boxing,' I said.

He touched his eyebrows. 'I can see the scars.'

'Don't let that fool you,' I said. 'I was just an amateur.'

He put his open hands up on either side of his head. 'I thought amateurs wore protective headgear.'

'We did, but sometimes things got personal and it was open slather. I cut easily. One reason why I never seriously considered being a professional.'

'Very wise. Okay, here's the thing you need to know and that will make two of us. I could be disciplined for telling you this but I reckon you're . . . what's the expression? . . . in Barry's corner.'

'I am.'

'Barry Bartlett can't be the father of the young man you spoke of. Barry's been sterile since birth.'

11

Dr Abrahams had had Barry as a patient around the time I had met him. He explained that Barry had so many endocrinal disturbances and malfunctions that he'd arranged a full hormonal screening.

'He was a mess,' Abrahams said. 'At first I thought it was just a lifestyle thing with some genetic factors thrown in, but it proved to be that in spades.'

He went on to explain that Barry had a hypothyroid condition that would have rendered him sterile but not impotent. He said that the condition could be controlled by drugs if it developed post-puberty but that its presence from birth ruled out any chance that Barry's sperm could have been fertile.

'I didn't tell him,' he said. 'What would have been the point? He was middle-aged with a lot of things to get under control. While the thyroid condition wouldn't have made him impotent the uncontrolled diabetes probably had, or near enough. He admitted to erectile problems and I didn't pursue it.'

Digesting this, I nodded.

'Do you have any children, Cliff?'

I shook my head.

'Any reason?'

'It was never an option.'

'I assumed it was the same with Barry. I knew a bit about him, of course. I knew he was a rascal, but I liked him. I assume you feel the same.'

'He has his good points.'

'I've broken some rules telling you this, but I respect Ian Sangster's judgement about a man and he rates you highly. You seem to be involved in a very delicate situation. I'll be frank with you. I don't think Barry has much of a chance. He's pretty much artificially maintained by medications as it is and every hour he spends in a coma will take a toll.'

'I'm sorry to hear that.'

'He did well to get this far. I can't control how you use this information, but I'm trusting you in two ways: one, not to reveal where you got it and two, to use it responsibly. As I say, I don't think it'll matter to Barry one way or the other.'

We shook hands again and I left. Doctors can disappoint or inspire. You're lucky if you're surprised in a good way.

*

Back at my office I called the hospital but there was no news on Barry. I tried Mountjoy's car and office numbers with no success, then on the home one I got his wife. Her strong American accent surprised me. She said she didn't know where her husband was. She hadn't heard from him since the morning. She asked me who I was and what my business was with Sir Keith. Her tone was unfriendly. I told her I was a private investigator making some enquiries for Sir Keith and BBE.

'That amateur bunch,' she said, 'I wish we'd never got involved with them. It wasn't necessary. What sort of enquiries?'

'I'm afraid I can't tell you that.'

'Oh, sure, how stupid of me. Private means private. Well, give me your name and number and I'll tell him you called.'

'Cliff Hardy. He has the number.'

'But you're the one who was involved in that disgusting greyhound business. I might have known he couldn't leave all that low-life crap alone. I suppose it's to do with a woman, or women. I have nothing more to say to you. Goodbye. Don't call here again.'

I made and ate a grilled ham and cheese sandwich and drank two glasses of cut-price red wine. In all probability Ronny wasn't Barry's son, but did Ronny know that? My guess was that he didn't. What did that imply for Ronny's future? Did Barry's will—if there was a new one—

simply name Ronny as his beneficiary or stipulate that his paternity had to be established before any legacy could take effect? With Barry in a coma, Ronny missing and Keith Mountjoy off somewhere unknown, my only way forward was through Senior Constable Bronwen Marr, aka Tania.

I took the earring from my pocket and laid it in my palm. It was a very small thing to rely on for progress in something growing ever more complicated.

I went to the gym in the morning and, to make the right impression on Ian Sangster, I was still in my gym gear when I caught him at his regular coffee break in Glebe Point Road. Coffee and cigarette break. Ian smoked twenty a day and ran marathons, arguing the one cancelled out the other. He looked me up and down.

'Commendable. Treadmill?'

'And weights. I just wanted to thank you for the introduction to Simon Abrahams.'

Ian was on his second long black with three sugars. He stirred the coffee. 'Don't know how you can stand the boredom of gym workouts. Helpful, was he?'

'Very. He's a credit to your profession.'

'Meaning he told you a whole lot of stuff he shouldn't have. I don't know how you manage to worm things out of people the way you do, Cliff.'

'Must be charm.'

He mimed looking around, up and down. 'I don't see it. Where d'you keep it?'

I thanked him again and watched him light a cigarette.

'What?' he said.

'Nothing.'

'I should think so. By the way, how is Barry Bartlett?'

'Crook, very crook.'

'A poor choice of words, mate. In my experience types like him get a few more years after the big scare. Just a few. I don't know why, it's another mystery to add to all the others. Like your survival. Take care, Cliff.'

There was no sign of the untrusting Lebanese waiter when, shaved, showered and hungry after the exercise, I got to the Bistro Beirut. I was wearing a white shirt, a navy sports coat and dark trousers. Slip-on Italian shoes, very old, very comfortable. I followed Ronny's example by ordering a beer and I surveyed the menu with genuine interest. All work and no play. Never an adventurous eater, I ordered the same meal as before. I poured and sipped the beer and watched as people tossed up whether go inside the restaurant or stay outside. The day was mild but the wind had an edge and the customers split about fifty-fifty.

She came just after my food arrived. She was wearing trousers, a rollneck sweater and a light jacket. Plenty of protection against the cool breeze and she didn't hesitate in taking an outside seat facing away from me. Her dark hair was medium length, brushed back at the sides, loose. She was taller than I'd first thought and more slender looking without the shoulder-padded suits. A waiter scurried eagerly towards her; a regular customer, possibly a good tipper. She placed her order and a glass of wine arrived inside a minute. I took the earring from my pocket, got up, took two steps and put it down beside her glass.

'Join me,' I said and resumed my seat.

She sat stock still for a moment, then turned to look at me. Recognition dawned. She took her shoulder bag from where she'd hooked it over the back of her seat, picked up her glass—and the earring—and sat at my table.

'Do I call you Bronwen or Tania?'

Her voice was husky, as I remembered. 'Don't call me anything. Just tell me who you are and what you want.'

The waiter arrived with her food. He hesitated, then brought it to my table, where I'd made sure there was space for it. She had a dish of olives, flat bread and felafel with baba ganoush.

'Light lunch,' I said and took in a solid forkful of chicken, hummus and tabouli.

She drank some wine and fiddled with the earring. Today she wasn't wearing earrings or any other kind of adornment. No makeup, flatties. She wasn't dressed for business or to seduce but there was something compelling about her strong features, hard mouth and calculating, green-eyed gaze. It wasn't something that happened to me often but now it did. I was suddenly intensely and disconcertingly attracted to her. I put the fork down and took a swallow of beer to cover my confusion.

'You haven't come here to discuss my lunch choice and it looks as though you aren't that interested in yours. What's this about?'

I didn't want the food or the beer, I just wanted to keep her there to look at her and hear her Lauren Bacall voice. All I wanted to do was hold her interest.

'Ronny Saunders,' I said. 'Aka Ronny Bartlett, except that he isn't.'

She was too well trained to be impressed or to react too obviously. She pursed her lips and took a bite of flat bread and a sip of wine.

'And who're you?'

I opened my wallet and showed her the PEA licence.

'Jesus, that's all I need. A dumb private eye.'

'Dumb?'

She picked up the earring and pushed back her hair. There were tiny, almost invisible studs in her ear lobes.

'My ears are pierced. This thing isn't mine.'

I sat back, looking, I'm sure, as dumb as I felt and as she thought me. She took pity on me.

'You're looking for him?' she said.

I nodded.

'Who for?'

I was so on the back foot in all ways that I couldn't do anything but answer honestly.

'Initially for Barry Bartlett and still for him while he's alive, but also for Sir Keith Mountjoy.'

She covered her face with her hands briefly and then removed them and looked around. She forked up some felafel, dabbled it in the dip and drank some wine. I finished my beer and gestured to the waiter to bring two more glasses of wine. I pushed the food around my plate and ate a little. The wine arrived. She finished her first glass and sipped the second.

'I admit I've made a mistake,' I said, 'but I had a reason. We have to exchange information. You know who I am. Who're you?'

She shook her head.

'I think you're an undercover policewoman investigating BBE and . . . its affiliates . . . for their involvement in something very important. Tell me I'm wrong.'

She drank some more wine. 'You're not so dumb after all,' she said.

'Thank you.'

'Go on with your guesswork.'

'You were instructed to get close to Ronald Saunders, aka Bartlett, in order to find out more about this big whatever-it-is. I saw you go about it very directly. Now Barry's in a coma and Ronny's in the wind, as the Yanks say. Your investigation's as stalled in its way as mine.'

94

'Are you suggesting we should be allies?'

I'd ally with you any day of the week, I thought. I loaded my fork with meat and hummus. 'Frank Parker's my oldest and closest friend,' I said. 'You could ring him and ask about me.'

'I can't go ringing up senior police officers to check on some roughneck private eye,' she said.

'Not so much of the roughneck. I introduced Frank to his wife, Hilde. They were there when he got the medal and so was I. So were you, looking at Parker as if he was the man of your dreams.'

'Was it that obvious?'

'Sorry, but yes, if you were sitting where I was.'

'Fuck,' she said.

12

She wanted to ask more questions but I insisted on some information first.

'Did I get it right about you?'

'Sort of. There's a new unit, small, a kind of offshoot, focused on corporate crime.'

'And you were detailed to get close to Ronny.'

She nodded.

'Did your lot plant him?'

Her eyes opened in surprise and I could see her remembering what I'd said about Ronny not being who she thought he was.

'Plant him? No, we'd had Bartlett in our sights for a while but he kept all his cards close to his chest. He didn't . . . provide any openings. Then the son turned up.'

'I don't suppose you'll tell me what sort of business you believe he's involved in?'

'No, but it's not a belief, it's certain knowledge.'

'Isn't it a nuisance when you have to provide proof? The things you have to do . . .'

'Bugger you. How can anyone in your sleazy game be so high and mighty? Anyway, let's stop insulting each other and see if we can be mutually useful instead. You say he's not Bartlett's son.'

I told her what Dr Abrahams had told me without revealing the source of the information.

'That was pretty good investigative work,' she said, 'if it's true. If it is, who is he?'

'I don't know. The physical resemblance isn't there now but I dug up some photos of Barry when young and it's very strong when you take away the years.'

She finished her wine and looked at me. 'When you take away the years . . . that's an interesting thing to say. I've underestimated you, Mr Hardy. They must be related, surely. This is confusing. Ron believes he's Bartlett's son, I think.'

'I agree with you. If he was just a doppelganger trying to hoodwink a wealthy man . . .'

'Or planted by someone, to use your expression.'

I nodded. 'He wouldn't be so convincing.'

We'd ignored the food and finished the wine and a waiter was lurking. She nodded at him and he cleared the table. That left us without any props or any real reason to stay where we were but it seemed neither of us wanted to move.

'Coffee?' I said.

'I don't like the coffee here. Let's go somewhere else. You can pay. I like the thought of Barry Bartlett or Keith Mountjoy paying for my lunch.'

She wasn't far short of my height in her flatties and she moved with a long, athletic stride. It was odd to be feeling such a strong attraction to someone about whom I knew almost nothing, not even what name she was currently using. Someone who'd sized me up as a dumb roughneck but now seemed to be having second thoughts. I was attracted but wary—an intense combination.

We went to a small café up the street and sat inside because a light rain had started to fall.

'You know this area, don't you?' I said. 'You live around here.'

She smiled. It was the first time I'd seen her smile and when she did the lips didn't seem so thin and her mouth looked more generous. 'You're detecting,' she said.

I shrugged. 'Habit.'

'You have to go to the counter to order and pay here. Mine's a latte, yours is a long back.'

She went to a red phone in the corner and made a call. Someone at the counter was chatting, forcing me to wait to order and pay, and I watched her at the phone as I waited. The call was brief and she went back to her seat.

I ordered, paid, came back and sat down at the small table. Our knees touched. The place was narrow, everything tightly packed. It was quiet in the early afternoon with only half a dozen other customers. Some vaguely Italian-sounding music was playing softly.

'Cards on the table,' she said. 'I didn't call Superintendent Parker, but someone else vouched for you. I'm sorry I insulted you.'

'It's all right. I'm sorry I assumed you slept with Ronny but it seemed logical at the time. I followed you back to his flat.'

'I see. Well, I didn't. He wanted to but I wasn't up for it . . . not then, anyway. We had an argument. He must have found other female company. It hardly matters.'

'No, the big question now is why he hasn't surfaced on hearing that Barry's so sick.'

She nodded. 'If he's heard. If he hasn't, that's a worry. We both have an interest in finding him.'

The coffee arrived. She ate the froth from her spoon; mine was too hot to sip.

'Not quite the same interest, though,' I said.

'No, that's a pity.'

'It's a question of how far apart they are,' I said. 'I was initially contracted to make sure Ronny wasn't a threat to Barry, now simply to find him. If Barry's involved in something very big and very criminal I'd be surprised but not too concerned. And the way things are it might not matter to him anyway. But you know the way things are, don't you?'

'Why do you say that?'

I drank some coffee. 'I'm sure you have access to the latest information from the hospital.'

'It comes by fax.'

'Is that right?'

She stirred her coffee, drank some and then pushed it away.

'Not as good as usual?' I said. 'Mine's okay.'

She'd dipped her head; now she lifted it and there were strain lines around her eyes that aged her. I'd judged her to be in her early thirties but she looked younger when relaxed. 'I've fucked this assignment up.'

'Is it your first undercover job?'

'It's that obvious?' She grimaced, then said, 'Can you find him?'

'Maybe, I have a few ideas. Look, I don't know what to call you. It's like talking to a shadow.'

She smiled and the strain lines disappeared. 'Poetic again. Bronwen, Bron.'

I put my hand across the table. 'Cliff.'

We shook. We were touching at two points, hands and knees.

'Okay, Cliff, the fax'll come through to my place, which is just around the corner, as you guessed. You'd follow me there anyway to find where I lived, wouldn't you?'

'A professional duty.'

'Let's go then.'

*

Her flat was in a large, high-security block in Lansdowne Street. We didn't speak on the short walk, both preoccupied with our thoughts. We took the lift to the fifth floor and went in to an open-plan studio flat with the sleeping, living, eating and working arrangements all on display—a single bed in a corner, a medium-sized pine table with four chairs, a coffee table with two saucer chairs and a large desk. Bookshelves had been arranged to give the desk something of a separate office feel. The kitchenette was partly partitioned off from the living space by a waist-high wall. There were large windows on two sides and a small balcony.

She shrugged out of her jacket and hung it on a hook near the door.

'Compact,' I said.

She nodded. 'Affordable.'

She moved to the working area, which consisted of a telephone with a fax and an answering machine. I went to where the windows gave a view towards Oxford Street and a slice of Hyde Park. If you liked looking down on an active business and residential part of your city, this was a good place to be. There were pot plants on the balcony that would catch the morning sun. One was a mandarin tree and the other was a flowering shrub of some kind.

I heard her tear the fax sheet loose. She came up behind me. It was cold in the room and I could feel the warmth of her body.

'Like the view, Cliff?' she said.

'I do.'

'Got one at your place?'

'Glimpse of Blackwattle Bay, between two blocks of flats.'

She laughed. 'Here's the news from the hospital. No change.'

'That's bad. The doctors tell me the longer he's in a coma the worse the likely result.'

The phone rang and she moved quickly away and picked up.

'God,' she said. 'Yes, yes, I'll be there.'

She stood, apparently shocked, still holding the receiver. I went to her, took it and replaced it.

'What is it?' I said.

'I have to go.'

'Was it Ronny?'

'No.'

'Bron, we're in this together in some sense. Tell me. What's happened?'

'Sir Keith Mountjoy's been found shot dead.'

13

Bron said she had a meeting with other members of the police intelligence team. I gave her my card and after some hesitation she gave me her telephone number at home and one where she could be contacted at what she called 'the unit'. We left the flat together and shook hands in the street.

'What're you driving?' I said.

She smiled. 'Wouldn't you like to know?'

I walked back to where I'd left the Falcon and drove to my office. A police car stood in St Peters Lane in violation of the parking rules. I eased mine into my private space. A plain-clothes cop and a uniform got out of the car and approached me.

'Cliff Hardy,' Plain-clothes said.

'The same.' Sometimes I just can't help myself with cops. This one looked suitably annoyed as he produced his warrant card.

'Detective-Sergeant Bruce O'Connor. I'd like to ask you a few questions.'

'In connection with what?'

'That can wait until we're somewhere we can talk.'

I looked up and down the lane and then up at the church wall that flanked it. 'I can talk here. There's no one listening.'

The uniform backed away, sensibly not wanting to be too close a witness to this byplay with his superior. O'Connor was tall and strongly built with a squarish Celtic face now flushing a little.

He sighed. 'I was warned you liked to play games, Hardy. Okay, here's a game for you: we go up to your office to talk or we take you to you-know-where.'

You have to know when to fold 'em. I jiggled my keys. 'The office it is. You'd better have the constable move the car or you'll get a ticket. The bulldogs are savage around here.'

O'Connor jerked his head at the uniform and followed me into the building and up the two flights of stairs to my office. The stairwell smelled of its age and the deterioration of the materials it was made of. I resisted the urge to test his wind on the stairs. I had my name and *PRIVATE ENQUIRIES* stencilled on the door and I was still unsure about the italics, and whether ENQUIRIES or INQUIRIES was better.

I unlocked the door and ushered O'Connor in to the one biggish room with its functional well-tested fittings, grimy windows and an untidiness suggestive, I claimed, of work being done rather than neglect. The truth was, I spent as

106

little time in the office as possible. I pointed to the client chair and settled myself behind the desk.

'Now, where were we?' I said.

'Why are you determined to piss me off?'

'It's a habit I've fallen into after some bad experiences with some of your colleagues.'

'It's a bloody bad habit.' He took out a notebook. 'I want you to account for your movements over the past eight hours.'

'I'll try to do that when you tell me what this is about. Otherwise I phone my lawyer and we all do the old foxtrot.'

He didn't want to do it but he wasn't a natural born bully like some of them. 'It's about the death of Sir Keith Mountjoy.'

'Ah.'

'What does that mean?'

'It means you or someone else has been talking to Lady Mountjoy and learned that I phoned her yesterday trying to contact her husband.'

He nodded. 'You're not her favourite person. Did you contact him?'

'No.'

'I know how tricky you are—did he contact you?'

'No.'

'All right. Back to the question of your whereabouts.'

'We're talking about, say, seven in the morning until now, right? Well, I went to the gym early, about eight, then I had a talk to my doctor in Glebe about this and that and went home for a shower and a shave and to put on the clothes you see me in now.'

He made a note. 'You're at it again. I don't give a shit about what you're wearing.'

'It's relevant; I could've changed out of the blood-spattered clothes.'

'Hardy . . .'

'I'm sorry. Then I had lunch with someone in Surry Hills. Lebanese place in Riley Street. You could check with the waiters.'

'Who did you lunch with?'

'I can't tell you that.'

What was he thinking? That I'd lunched with the killer and congratulated him, or paid him? Any speculation was possible for a policeman this early in an investigation. It didn't matter. I couldn't tell him about Bronwen for her sake and, I realised, for my own.

He made a note and looked around the room.

'D'you want to see my pistol? It's not here. It's at home under lock and key as required.'

'Not necessary. Mountjoy was killed by a sawn-off shotgun at close range.'

'Haven't used a shottie in years.'

With an effort he relaxed his hard, serious face into something like a smile. 'Any ideas about who might have had it in for Mountjoy?'

I shrugged. 'He wasn't the most popular guy in town. I had the impression his wife didn't like him all that much.'

'There's that,' he said. 'And what can you tell me about your asking where he was?'

As cops go, O'Connor wasn't terrible and I didn't feel like baiting him anymore. 'I'm conducting an investigation for Barry Bartlett. Barry's out of action, as you might have heard. Mountjoy was sort of filling in for him and I was . . . liaising with him.'

'Nice company you keep.'

'There's worse.'

'That's true.' He put the notebook away and stood. 'You're what we call a person of interest.'

'I'm flattered.'

'Don't be. We might have to dance that foxtrot some time.'

He left, closing the door quietly. I hadn't made a friend, but I wouldn't have counted him as one of my enemies. I didn't know much about Mountjoy other than his earlier involvement in the greyhound business and what I'd learned lately, but he had a rough diamond look about him. The shotgun suggested criminal involvement of a rougher brand than those usually associated with corporate crime. My problem with this case now was, with Barry out of action and Mountjoy dead, I didn't have a client.

*

But I did have another case, and another client, and I set off for Little Bay. It went down pretty much as Zac had predicted at Botany Security. I got through the gate, trying to give the guard a good look at the pass but he was focused on a big woman in high heels and a red power suit approaching behind me. Zac, waiting at a vantage point, made his call and as I waited at the steps leading up to the office block an executive type came out looking flustered. We didn't speak; he just eyeballed me, took the pass and returned inside. I walked back through the gate and this time I did see alarm on the face of the guard.

Zac's van was parked beside my Falcon and I joined him there.

'Sweet,' Zac said.

'I suppose so.'

'What's wrong? The cheque'll be in the mail this arvo.'

'I dunno. Just a feeling.'

'You just don't like big business.'

'True. Are they big business?'

Zac rubbed his hands. 'Getting bigger, they tell me.'

The evening TV news bulletins carried the details of Mountjoy's murder. He'd been shot in his car when it was drawn up at a petrol station in Randwick in the mid-morning. It was a self-serve place and, according to the attendant who was inside the station paying-point and shop at the time, someone had walked up, fired and walked away.

Visuals showed that the attendant would have been at least thirty metres away from the event and with a view partly obscured by Mountjoy's car, a sleek convertible I couldn't identify. His description of the shooter amounted to no more than 'a big ordinary-looking guy. Not black or Asian.'

As I switched off the television I remembered a story I'd heard years before about a woman who'd fallen onto the tracks at Central Station with a train approaching. Someone had jumped down, lifted her back to the platform and disappeared into the crowd. When interviewed later about the identity of her rescuer she could only describe him as 'Some wog.'

We're multicultural now but some are more multicultural than others.

I was thinking about food without much enthusiasm when the phone rang.

'Hardy at home.'

'This is Bron, out in the fucking world. I have to talk to someone. Can I come and see you?'

'Sure you can.'

'Are you alone?'

Very much so, I thought. 'Yes.'

'I know you said Glebe. What's the address?'

I told her and she said she'd be with me in under half an hour. I hung up and thought about tidying the living room and didn't, remembering the state of her own place. I rinsed a few dishes and stacked them in the drainer.

I had half a dozen eggs, a couple of onions, a wilted capsicum and a tomato. I could make one of my specialties— a chilli omelette. I had an unopened bottle of Bombay Sapphire gin and some tonic water. No lemon. Two bottles of generic white.

The doorbell rang. She stood in the dim porch light still in the clothes she'd been wearing earlier, with a scarf for a bit of extra warmth. No glasses.

'Hi,' she said.

'Come in.'

'A house. All yours?'

'Mostly. The bank has a bit of it. Come through. Would you like a drink? I've got gin, whisky and wine.'

'A G&T would be great.'

'No lemon.'

'I wouldn't mind if there was no tonic even.'

We went through to the kitchen where you could sit in reasonable comfort around a benchtop. She hung her bag on a door handle, her jacket and scarf on the back of a chair and sat while I prepared the drinks.

'A single man in a place this size,' she said. 'I'm guessing you weren't always single.'

'That's right. Have been for a while though. Just can't think of anywhere else I'd rather be.'

I made two strong drinks and sat down opposite her. She touched glasses and took a long swallow.

'That hits the spot.'

'Tough meeting?'

'As always. I'm the only woman. What've you been doing since we were together?'

'I was interviewed by the police about Mountjoy's murder.'

'Why?'

I explained the background and she listened intently. We worked on our drinks. She'd seemed to be trying to relax and wasn't doing very well at it until the gin started to help. She drank quickly and rattled the ice cubes.

'Refill?'

'Better not. Got anything to eat? I'm starving.'

I made the omelette, halved it and served it with toast then poured the cheap wine. She ate and drank quickly, nervous again. She finished and wiped her mouth with a tissue from a box on the table.

'I needed that.'

I laughed. 'Well, you didn't have much lunch.'

She smiled. 'I'm nervous.'

'I noticed. More wine?'

'Just a touch. How did things go with the police?'

'I convinced Detective O'Connor I hadn't killed Sir Keith Mountjoy with a shotgun. What happened at your meeting to upset you?'

'They told me I had to find Ronald Saunders and I said I would although I had no fucking idea how to do it except one—through you.'

'So that's why you're here?'

'Not entirely.'

We stood and moved together. I put my arms around her and felt her hands on my shoulders, drawing me closer. We kissed tentatively and then again, harder. She tasted of wine and chilli and her lips didn't feel thin. Her body felt strong and eager and my response was immediate. She spoke in her husky voice close to my ear.

'I had a feeling that you liked me.'

'What gave you that idea?'

'Little things and one big thing—you were glad I hadn't fucked Ronald.'

'You're right,' I said.

14

Upstairs she peeled off her sweater and undid her bra to reveal very small, very firm breasts. She took my hands and placed them so that they covered her breasts completely.

'Are you a tit man?' She pressed against me. 'Oh, I see that you are.'

After that it was frantic—a tugging at zips, a scramble for a condom—and physical, our teeth clashing, our knees giving way. She was thin; her hip bones dug into me as we locked together. I didn't care. She whispered things I couldn't hear for the roaring in my ears. I came too quickly despite trying not to and she thrust up hard, gripping and grinding until she let out a series of groans and fell back.

Somehow we ended up side by side still joined.

'Sorry,' I said, 'I was too quick. It'd been a while.'

She eased away and we separated. 'Didn't matter. I got there.'

I ran my hands down her body.

'I know I'm skinny,' she said. She felt the flesh at my waist. 'Not bad for your age. No love handles to speak of. Do you go to the gym?'

'Not as often as I should.' I traced the lines of her shoulder bones. 'I'm guessing you're a runner.'

'Hurdler,' she said.

I kissed her. 'A veritable gazelle.'

'More poetry. I can't work you out, Cliff.'

The bed had been unmade when we hit it, with a wrinkled bottom sheet now slipping towards the floor. Without too much disturbance I pulled up the top sheet and blanket and adjusted us so we were as comfortable as if we'd done this a hundred times before. Comfortable physically, but with everything else up for grabs.

'I'm going to have to sleep for a while,' she said. 'Have you got another rubber?'

'Mmm.'

'In the morning.'

Eight am found us sexually satisfied, her in my kimono which was a present from a lover of some time back and me in a towelling bathrobe that had somehow got into my luggage after a hotel stay. We were drinking coffee, eating toast and marmalade and not looking our best. I was heavily stubbled and Bron's face and other parts of her were roughened from my bristles.

She smeared marmalade on a third piece of toast, ate it and sipped coffee. 'You fuck better than you make coffee.'

'I hope so. My coffee always turns out bitter.'

She looked at me before she took a bite. 'Is that supposed to mean something?'

'Not at all. I'm not that metaphorical.'

She nodded and drank some coffee. 'It's not that bad anyway. Are you going to help me find Ronald or . . . ?'

'Find whatever happened to him.'

'I was going to say find out what he might have done.'

She'd had the same thought as me. Without any real reason to think so, it had crossed both our minds that Ronny might have killed Sir Keith. It wasn't a strong suspicion for me. The garage attendant had described the shooter as big, but he was a weedy little number who might see all average-sized people as big. But the thought was there, and we still didn't really know who Ronny was or what his agenda might be.

'Can you tell me what it is your intelligence unit is looking into with BBE?'

'I can't, Cliff. I just can't. I'm more or less on probation in the unit as it is. If I told you and it came out, that'd be the finish for me. I'd be back in uniform at least, if not off the force.'

'O'Connor asked me who I was with at lunch yesterday. I didn't tell him. Doesn't that count for anything?'

She reached out and touched my hand. 'Thank you, but no.'

'I see.'

'So you won't help.'

'I didn't say that, but we'll have to strike a deal. If we find Ronny you have to agree to let me talk to him first.'

'So you've got an idea.'

'Just one, a long shot.'

The kimono had fallen open and I could see her breasts. She saw me looking and covered herself. 'Okay, it's a deal. What's the idea?'

'The last person we know of who saw Ronny was a woman who left her earring in his bed.'

Bron nodded. 'A hooker. Just how many are there in Sydney, would you say?'

'He's disappointed that you've gone and he's randy. He's had an argument with his father later in the day. He wants female company. What's he likely to do?'

'You tell me.'

'Get someone local who'd be there quickly. He'd be eager, and after missing out on you he wouldn't go looking in the street. He'd want something classier.'

'Thanks. How many brothels in Paddo?'

'A few, probably, but maybe we can narrow it down if there's a redial function on his phone. I've still got the keys.'

We went in two cars, hers a newish-looking Audi. People had left for work and we were able to park reasonably close and not too far apart.

'The rent'd be steep,' Bron said as we went up the stairs.
'Barry owns the block.'

'The wages of sin.'

The place was exactly as it had been when I'd last inspected it. Bron eyed the empty Great Western champagne bottle and the plastic glasses.

'Funny,' she said, 'it feels like a crime scene but it isn't, is it?'

'Hope not.' I took out a notebook and a pen and sat down by the phone.

'Hold on,' Bron said. 'It's not even ten o'clock. Would they be answering?'

'Depends on their MO. Some places are round-the-clock, but if they aren't they have an answering machine.'

'Hit it,' she said.

I pressed redial and poised my pen. The voice that came on the line had the breathy, fruity tones of the profession, the vowels overproduced and the pitch low: *You have called the Paddington Pussies but we're afraid you'll have to wait. We know you will. Please call back after six for what will be an evening to remember.*

Bron was already leafing through the *Yellow Pages*. She held out the open page—a big spread extolling the qualities of young, exotic escorts. 'This is it, Raleigh Crescent, off Oxford Street. What now?'

We were both on our feet, me putting away my notebook and her letting go of the directory. I reached out for her but she held me back. 'What now?' she repeated.

The tension between us was palpable. 'This is my territory, not yours,' I said. 'You tell your people, whoever they are, you have a line of enquiry. I'll contact you when I learn anything.'

'What do you mean by "whoever they are"?'

'I've had a lot of experience with police, Bron. There's good and bad among them; there's certainly discreet and indiscreet.'

'You don't trust me.'

'I *want* to trust you.'

'That's all?'

'For now.'

'I'm glad we came in our own cars.' She turned abruptly and walked out.

I found a plastic bag in a kitchen drawer and put the smeared glass in it.

The tenant in flat one opened the door as I was leaving the building. He was back in his dressing gown. A gentleman of leisure.

'How is he, our lord and master?'

'He's in a coma.'

'God, and this used to be such a quiet building.'

'And not now?'

'Well, not after that drama and the kerfuffle the night before.'

'What was that?'

He told me that he'd been aware of strange noises on the stairs late on that evening and that when he'd looked out his window he saw two men escorting the young man who'd not long moved in upstairs out to a car.

'I assumed, you know, police, drugs. I kept my head down I can tell you.'

I showed him my PEA licence and said I was working for his landlord and asked if he could describe the men.

'Oh, I only saw their backs, actually. One was big, I mean *really* big, the way some of them are. Then the . . . young woman left a little later.'

'And she was . . . ?'

He shrugged elegantly. 'A professional, I'd say. Not that I have any experience in that particular field.'

I went back to the office to find a message on the answering machine.

'Mr Hardy, this is Simon Abrahams. I've had a message from the hospital that Barry Bartlett is awake and communicating. I'm tied up for the morning but if you're going to see him you might tell him I'll come in as soon as possible. I left the message, but some personal reinforcement would help.'

I was pleased on a number of counts. I had some time for Barry despite his chequered past and the signs that he was currently involved in something problematical. And because I had a client again. St Vincent's was a walk away and I didn't stop for flowers or grapes.

Barry had been moved out of Intensive Care into a private room. I asked if anyone else had been to see him and was told Mr Templeton had just left. I was advised to make my visit short and not to upset the patient.

'You tough old bastard,' I said as I walked in and found Barry propped up against a heap of pillows. 'You should be dead.'

'Look who's talking,' he said. 'Gidday, Cliff, they tell me I was lucky to have someone with a cool head on the spot. Thanks.'

'The guy in number one helped. You might let him off a month's rent, or two months.'

He nodded. 'I'll do that.'

'Well, they've kept you alive until you decided not to throw in the towel. You boxed on, Barry. Doc Abrahams asked me to tell you he'll be in as soon as he can.'

Barry was newly pale and his face had become drawn. His expression was hard to interpret with the new appearance. He smiled but the smile was slightly crooked. Looked as though the seizure had left some telltale traces.

'Cy Abrahams! You've seen him?'

'Wanted to know whether to write you off as a client or not.'

'Fuck you. What did he tell you?'

A moment of truth, but I dodged it. 'Medical stuff. Didn't understand half of it. You're going to have to make some changes . . .'

THAT EMPTY FEELING

'Yeah, yeah, I know. What about Ronny? Have you found him?'

I had plenty of material to upset him with: his non-paternity, Ronny's abduction, Keith Mountjoy—but, in the hospital gown with the pale blue pillows supporting him, he seemed fragile.

'Still looking,' I said. 'But I've got a lead.'

15

Paddington Pussies was open for business when I arrived at 7 pm. The wide three-storey terrace had a high front wall and a security gate. A low hum told me pressing the buzzer had activated a camera. I was wearing the suit I'd worn to Barry's party and was freshly shaved and barbered. I had the jacket unbuttoned so the bagged glass in the pocket didn't make an unsightly bulge. Evidently I passed muster because the heavy gate swung open. I went up a well-maintained tiled path to an equally neatly tiled porch. A door painted bright red stood open.

I went in. There was a carpeted central lobby with an ornate desk in the middle and behind that a wide staircase. The woman behind the desk was an impeccably made-up blonde in her forties showing three inches of deep cleavage. There was a white telephone on the desk, an ashtray with a gold packet of Benson & Hedges cigarettes and a gold lighter. Also a switch with a cable leading from it. Muted concealed strip lighting was kind to her.

'Good evening, sir. How may we help you?'

It was the sculptured voice I'd heard on the answering machine. I showed her my licence. 'You can help me with some information.'

She raised one plucked eyebrow. 'Oh?'

'About who serviced a client who phoned a few nights ago from an address in Paddington.'

'I don't think so.'

'I'm pretty sure I could find some drugs in this establishment and I wouldn't be surprised to turn up an under-age girl or two.'

Her manicured hand with long, scarlet fingernails moved to the switch.

'Go ahead. Call him. We'll have a chat.'

She pressed the switch and after a couple of minutes a man came down the stairs. He wore a suit over a rollneck skivvy. He was about my size, perhaps a bit bigger. He had a shaven head and wore a silver earring. He moved to the side of the desk.

'Trouble, Hannah?'

I showed him the licence. 'Shouldn't be. I want to talk to one of your girls.' I put my hand in my pocket and produced the earring. 'She left this behind. I want to return it.'

'Said he wanted information, Luke,' Hannah said, her voice now not so modulated.

Luke shook his head. 'Piss off,' he said.

'We can do this the quiet way or the noisy way,' I said. 'But it's going to be done. Be smart and no one gets hurt. Business as usual.'

He took a brass knuckle-duster from his pocket, slipped it onto his left hand and came around the desk. I had two advantages—I knew what his first punch would be like and anyone moving sideways and forward is momentarily off balance.

My straight left came before he was properly set. As Sally Brewer said, fighting a southpaw starts with the footwork. I had my feet in the right position and my weight properly distributed. I ducked under the punch and hooked hard to his ribcage. He sagged against the desk and I hit him again, lower. The wind went out of him and he held onto the desk with both hands. The knuckle-duster fell into Hannah's lap. I took hold of his earring, twisted it and he yelped.

'Give me any trouble and I'll rip it out. Okay, now that's all the rough stuff there needs to be. Hannah—Carstairs Street in Paddington on Monday night.'

I'd thought about Ronny's movements that night. It was about eight o'clock when he left the pub. Give him time to get to Barry's, have an argument and go home again and think about being lonely and randy.

'Some time around ten,' I said, 'name of Ronny. Who?'

It had all happened very quickly. Hannah was still staring at big Luke gasping for breath and squirming with my hand to his ear.

'C . . . Cindy.'

'I want her down here now! Just for a few words. Then I'm off and there's no blood spilt. Right, Luke?'

He was game enough to take the chance as I knew he would be. He pulled free and swung but I was ready and I drove my knee into his groin and he went down screaming, catching the side of his naked head on the edge of the desk as he fell. I pointed to a couch by the wall a few yards to the side.

Hannah punched buttons on the phone. 'Cindy, down to the desk, darling. Right now.'

'Listen, Hannah, Cindy and I'll be over there. You and Luke stay here.'

She looked down at the man with the bleeding head. He was clutching his crotch.

'We thought he was tough,' she said.

'He might be, but he doesn't get enough practice. With me, it's a full-time job.'

Cindy came down the stairs—high heels, short skirt, long legs, tight top, big hair. She stopped a few steps up.

'It's okay, darling,' Hannah said. 'No problems. This . . . gentleman wants a word.'

Cindy's voice was high-pitched and frightened. 'What's wrong with Luke?'

I beckoned for her to come down. 'He tripped and fell. Don't worry, I'll keep my distance. Just a few questions.'

Her kohl-rimmed eyes widened and she looked at Hannah, who nodded. She came down and I ushered her across to the couch. She sat and I stood. She was in her early twenties, quite pretty but vacant-eyed. She summoned up a professional smile.

'Have you got a cigarette?'

'No, and you wouldn't have time to smoke it. You went to Paddington on Monday night. Saw a guy named Ronny. You left this behind.'

I produced the earring. She nodded and looked very worried. She shot a glance at Hannah.

'I know what happened,' I said. 'Two men came and took him away.'

'Yes, I was bloody scared, like now.'

'No need to be scared now, Cindy,' I said in what I hoped was a reassuring voice. 'All I want to know is how Ronny was, how the men got in, what they said and what they looked like. I know a bit about it so don't lie to me.'

My attempt to be soothing hadn't worked in my favour. Instead, she'd found a new level of confidence.

'Fuck you! I'm not telling you anythink.'

I took the bagged glass from my pocket and showed it to her. 'Cindy, this isn't a police matter yet but it might be. That flat could be a crime scene, an abduction. This has your fingerprints on it. And puts you there. How would you feel about talking to the cops?'

The bravado left her. 'I didn't do nothink,' she said.

129

'I know you didn't. Answer my questions and you can take this and throw it away.'

She reached for the bag but I moved it. She glanced across at the desk. Luke had gone.

'What were the questions again? I've forgotten.'

'How was Ronny before the men came in?'

She couldn't help herself, grinned. 'He was horny.'

'He paid you?'

'Course he did. Up front. What d'you think? He was a good fuck, too.'

'I'm glad to hear it. Now, how did the men get in?'

Cindy wasn't the brightest or her wits had been dulled by something. 'How do you mean?'

'Did they knock at the door?'

'They just walked in.'

'So they had a key?'

She shrugged. 'I suppose.'

'Okay, what did they say?'

'I forget. Not much.'

'Did Ronny resist? I mean fight them? Were you up and dressed by then?'

'Yeah, he wanted to go out somewhere. He'd put his coat and scarf and that on, but I told him I had to get back to work.'

I waited for her to go on. She clearly had difficulty holding two thoughts in her head at the same time. 'What did you ask again?'

'Did he resist?'

'Shit, he tried. He stepped in front of me like, and he pushed the little guy away but the big one hit him and he fell over. Then they sort of picked him up and took him out.'

'You can't remember anything they said?'

She shook her head.

'What did they call him?'

She thought. 'Ronny.'

'What did they call each other?'

'Huh?'

'Did the big one call the smaller one anything or vice-versa?'

'Yeah, the big one said, "You're a weak prick, Titch," after Ronny pushed him away. He called him Titch. Titch got real angry. I was fuckin' scared. Gimme the glass.'

'In a minute. This is important. Describe them. The little one first.'

'Like a fuckin' jockey. Real little with a big nose. Never seen him before but I know the type. Some of them have big pricks.'

'The big one?'

She put her hand to her face. 'He had one of them . . . what're they called? Sort of blotches.'

'Birthmarks.'

'Yeah. Red. Real ugly.'

I handed her the glass and the earring.

16

Busy day and not done yet. I didn't know who Titch was but big, with a key and a port-wine birthmark had to be Des O'Malley. Barry had given me his direct line in the hospital and I rang it from a public phone.

'Hardy, you bastard. You didn't tell me Keith Mountjoy was dead.'

'I was instructed not to upset you. Does it upset you, Barry?'

'Yes and no. Shit, things are going to get out of hand while I'm stuck in here and they tell me I'll have weeks of . . . what d'they call it?'

'Convalescence.'

'Yeah, fuck that. How are you going with finding my boy?'

Still not the time to tell him, I thought. 'It looks as if Des had something to do with it.'

'Des? I can't believe it. He's been with me for years.'

'*Et tu, Brute.* I reckon he's been a snake in the grass for years, too. Where does he live, Barry?'

'He's got a house across the street from me in Randwick. Number twelve. Little joint.'

'Do you own it?'

'No. Des came out of boxing with a bit of dough but not much. He bummed around for a while, doing odd jobs, security and that, until I took him on. I helped with the deposit on his house and I pay him enough for him to keep up with the mortgage. I can't believe he . . .'

'What does he do for you?'

Barry's trust in me only went so far. 'This and that,' he said. 'What're you going to do?'

'I'm not sure. I'm in the dark here, Barry. You know the cops're keeping an eye on you and BBE.'

'Have for years. I suppose you got that from your mate, Parker.'

'No, from another source. And Sir Keith must've been involved in something big to finish the way he did. What is it? Can you tell me? I want to find Ronny for you but I'm stumbling around not knowing the big picture.'

I could imagine him chafing at the inactivity, confined to his hospital bed with tubes attached. Having been in that condition myself a few times I knew that nothing short of amputation can make you feel so helpless. The receiver was greasy and the phone box smelled of cigarette smoke.

'It *is* big,' Barry said at last. 'Very big. It's to do with petrol.'

One link forged perhaps: Mountjoy had been killed at a petrol station. 'That could be federal,' I said.

'It is. I'm tired, Cliff. These drugs are rooting me. Just find Ronny and get him clear. Sky's the limit, money-wise.'

He hung up and I got out of the foul box as quickly as I could. I couldn't remember when I'd last eaten and I could feel my blood-sugar level was low. My totally irresponsible diabetic mother had forced me to be aware of such things. Low sugar equals slow thinking. I found a café in Oxford Street and ordered a BLT with chips. I stirred two spoonfuls of sugar into the coffee and closed my mind down while I ate and drank.

Despite what I'd said to Des O'Malley at the BBE party, going up against him wasn't a thing to take lightly. He'd be a much tougher proposition than Titch whoever-he-was. I'd seen O'Malley fight and knew he was very good. He could have been better but he fell into bad habits, mainly gambling, which caused him to make money at boxing the dirty way. He was overweight now but he'd still have the moves.

The night was young and the time to tackle Des was late, when he'd had a drink or two and was tired. I went home for my gun.

'Hello, Cliff.' Bron stepped out from the shadow on the porch cast by the severely neglected rubber tree.

'Jesus!'

'You're slipping. You should have spotted the Audi.'

She was right. Her car was parked in clear view on the other side of the street.

'You looked purposeful until I scared you. What's going on?'

I unlocked the door.

'Are you going to ask me in?'

I nodded. 'We need to talk.'

We went inside. She was wearing a blue dress with a linen jacket and medium-heeled shoes. I took off my suit jacket and dropped it on a chair. I'd already taken off the tie. I went to the cupboard under the stairs and reached into a deep zipped pocket in a denim jacket and took out my .38 in its shoulder holster. She put her bag down on the coffee table and leaned against a bookshelf.

I had a cleaning kit with the gun and I sat and proceeded to strip and clean it. She watched sceptically. 'What's this supposed to prove?'

'Nothing,' I said. 'I think I know who grabbed Ronny and I'm going to pay him a visit. He'll probably need persuading.'

'Do you think Ronald will be there?'

'I don't know. Maybe.'

'I want to come.'

'Not a chance unless you tell me more about your involvement.'

She shook her head.

I didn't look up from what I was doing. 'Let me help you. Barry Bartlett, Sir Keith Mountjoy, BBE and Christ knows who or what else are involved in some large-scale operation about petrol. A lot of the things about petrol—excise, transportation, price, security—are federal matters. It's all a big deal since the oil crisis of a while back.'

She didn't react. I reassembled the pistol, loaded it and replaced it in the holster. I held up my hands. 'Have to wash up.'

She followed me out to the bathroom. I ran the hot tap, used the soap and grabbed a towel while still talking. 'I don't think you're a member of a gimcrack state police unit, Bron. I think you're either National Intelligence or Federal Police. How am I doing?'

Her voice was just above a whisper. 'Federal, on secondment.'

'Thanks.'

We went back to the kitchen and I held up the bottle of gin. She nodded and I made two moderate-strength drinks.

'We're not on opposite sides, Cliff.'

'Not exactly, but not quite on the same team either. You want to use Ronny to get information about this business. Long-term project. First off I wanted to vet him for Barry; now I just need to find him.'

'You did the first job—you found out he wasn't Bartlett's son.'

'Right, but I haven't told Barry yet. Did you tell your people that?'

'Yes.'

'Did you tell them about me?'

She shook her head.

'Why not?'

She knocked back some of her drink. 'I . . . I wanted to keep it separate if I could. I really like you; fuck it, I more than like you. I'm conflicted.'

So was I. We sat looking at each other, nursing the drinks that were inadequate for the moment. Physically and emotionally I liked everything about her, but trust was another matter.

She must have been thinking the same thing. 'The suit,' she said. 'You went to the brothel. That's how you got your lead. You weren't going to tell me, were you?'

'I wasn't sure.'

'You still haven't.'

'No. How about you—the dress, the shoes?'

She finished her drink. 'I wanted to look good for you.'

It takes a stronger man, more confident of his attractiveness than me, to resist something like that. We were out of our seats almost simultaneously and kissing. She grabbed me so fiercely I had to steady myself against the bench. It seemed like minutes before we broke apart.

'Let's find the little bugger,' I said, 'and decide what to do after that.'

17

The pact was unspoken but sealed. I went upstairs and changed into more workaday clothes. When I came down Bron was examining a Glock she'd taken from her bag.

'Never fired in anger,' she said.

'Let's keep it that way.' I strapped on the underarm holster. 'This one, too.'

'Which car?' she said.

'Yours. Des O'Malley, the guy we're calling on, might know mine and we could lose the element of surprise.'

I gave her the address and settled into the passenger seat, comfortable after I'd adjusted it. She drove in an expert but not flashy style and seemed to know her way around Alexandria and the easiest way to Randwick. I realised as I sat beside her that I knew almost nothing personal about her.

'You're a Sydney girl,' I said, 'from your knowledge of the geography.'

'That's right, Bronte.'

'Brick. A step up from me. I'm fibro, Maroubra.'

'And proud of it.'

'Yeah, I suppose.'

'Tell me about this O'Malley.'

'You've seen him. He was the guy on the door at the BBE party.'

She touched the side of her face.

'Other side, but that's him.'

I told her about O'Malley's history and Barry's surprise that he would be anything but loyal. I mentioned the man called Titch and then a thought struck me and I let out a grunt.

'What?'

'You're the one who looks out for cars. Ronny's ute wasn't at the flats when we looked there, was it?'

'No, definitely not.'

'Then O'Malley or Titch must have driven it away. They must have restrained Ronny in some way. It's not good, Bron. Utes . . .'

'You don't have to spell it out. Utes are good for dumping stuff.'

Barry's house, where I'd been a couple of times after fights, was built of sandstone, almost a mansion, set on a big corner block. It was surrounded by a high brick wall and had a security gate across the driveway. O'Malley's place across the road was a narrow detached cottage with no obvious security apparatus, which didn't mean there wasn't any. We cruised past it and parked in a side street about a hundred yards away.

'No sign of the ute close by,' Bron said. 'I wonder what that means.'

'It could mean it was used to dump Ronny and is now sitting torched somewhere in the Blue Mountains.'

She looked at me.

'Joking,' I said.

'Shit. How do we handle this?'

'What did they teach you in cop school?'

She swivelled in her seat and I could feel her eyes boring into me. 'Why're you being like that?'

'I'm sorry. I'm worried about you being here. I feel responsible for you and it doesn't help . . . planning.'

'Bugger you. I can do whatever's necessary.'

I remembered how she'd conducted herself at the siege. 'I know you can. I'm sorry.'

'Stop saying you're sorry and come up with a plan.'

'Two options—barge in at the front or scout along the lane at the back and get in that way if we can. Which do you like?'

'I get a vote, do I? The back. We can check for lights and movement and security.'

'How about I send you in the front looking gorgeous and you dazzle old Des or little Titch with your beauty?'

'You're doing it again.'

'The back it is.'

I'd brought a torch, a short jemmy and a lock pick.

'Illegal,' Bron said.

'You bet. I'm worried about your heels, much and all as I like the look of you in them.'

She reached over to the back seat for a sports bag, took out a pair of sneakers and, with the sort of flexibility I could only envy, shed the shoes and put on the sneakers.

We left the car doors unlocked and the keys on a shelf immediately under the ignition in case we needed a fast getaway. The lane behind the houses was festooned with NO PARKING signs but it was evidently rubbish pick-up time the next morning and there were one or two wheelie-bins outside most of the back gates. O'Malley's place was four houses along. It had a roller door that didn't quite meet the side fence and only one bin.

'I don't see Des as a recycler,' I said.

'Shut up, you're making me nervous with the wisecracks.'

She tested the stability of the bin, took one step back and sprang up onto the top of it and looked over the gap between the roller door and the fence.

'What?' I said.

She whispered, 'First, no dog. No light at the back. Easy drop to the yard.'

'If I can get up where you are. Getting a bit stiff in the joints these days.'

She disappeared over the gap, landing with barely a sound. I used a stray milk crate to clamber onto the wheelie-bin and heaved myself over the fence without too much trouble or noise. As we approached the back of the house a sensor light came on and we ducked into the shadows, but there was no further activity.

The porch had been built in and fitted with a screen door. I used the torch but couldn't see any signs of an alarm system and the screen door and the solid one behind it opened easily and quietly. The door to the kitchen stood open and I could hear the hum of the refrigerator motor but no other sound.

A light was showing in one of the rooms beyond the kitchen. We moved towards it with our pistols in our hands. The Smith has a double-pull safety and I hoped Bron's was similarly secured. She moved with no more sound than a shadow on a wall. The short passage led to a living room with its door ajar enough to allow the light to seep out, as well as a low moaning sound. I gestured to Bron to move the door open with her foot and then step back to let me in first.

The room was a shambles of overturned furniture, broken glass and the acrid smell of spilt blood. A man was sitting slumped against a wall. A very small man. His stumpy legs stretched out in front of him were twitching and he was making choked murmuring sounds. One side of his white shirt was dark with blood; he was sitting in a pool of it that had flowed from the wound and was still seeping.

Bron went straight into action. She shoved her gun into her bag, bent over the wounded man and unfastened his shirt, then took a packet of tissues from her bag, ripped it apart and made a thick wad that she pressed against the wound. The pad immediately darkened.

'Find a phone,' she said.

'I want to talk to him.'

'Jesus, Cliff . . .'

'He's finished, most of his blood's on the floor.'

Titch, it had to be him, gave a gasp. The blood-soaked pad fell away and a gout of blood flowed. A section of green-grey intestine bulged from the wound. Bron turned away, retching.

'What happened, Titch?' I said. 'Did you take Ronny Bartlett?'

The use of his name seemed to energise him, as if he knew it was the last time he'd hear it.

'Yeah. We fucked up.'

'Who? . . . And where've you stashed Ronny?'

'It all went wrong. I got shanked . . . Some bastards broke in and fuckin' Des got out fast. Left me here to fuckin' die.'

And that's what he did. He tried to suck in a breath but blood welled up into his mouth and his head fell sideways. The ugly gash in his belly stopped oozing as his heart ceased its pumping. Bron had recovered and was squatting, watching. I helped her to her feet.

'We have to get out of here,' I said.

'We can't. He . . .'

'He's out of it, but we're not. Do you want to explain what you're doing here to the local cops? What you're doing cooperating with someone like me? How're your federal colleagues going to take that?'

'You're a bastard.'

'When I have to be. This is for your sake as well as mine. I'll call this in anonymously when we get clear. That's the best we can do for him.'

She nodded. 'How do we leave?'

'The way we came in.'

I took a handkerchief from my pocket and folded the blood-soaked pad into it. She looked at me as if I'd broken wind in her face.

'You weren't here,' I said, 'and neither was I.'

18

I drove. I made the call from a phone box in Alison Road. I got back in the car and found Bron giving me a hard stare.

'You've done that before,' she said.

'Made anonymous phone calls? Sure.'

'Had men die in front of you and not been upset.'

'Who says I wasn't upset?'

'Didn't seem to be.'

'At times like that you have to think clearly. Being upset doesn't help. If we'd stayed until the police came I'd have been more upset and so would you. Bleeding to death from a stab wound isn't the worst way out. The shock deals with the pain. You're right, I've seen it before in the army, and if you're upset the next thing you're likely to be is dead.'

'Okay.'

I put my arm around her and she leaned against me and

we sat there, illegally parked, while cars flashed by us, some honking in protest. A loud blast from a bus roused her.

'I'm okay,' she said. 'We'd better move. Let's go to my place and think about where we are now with this mess.'

I drove to Surry Hills. She used the remote control device to access the underground carpark and we rode the lift up to her floor. She carried her bag and her shoes. I carried the jemmy, the torch, the lock pick and the blood-soaked wad of tissues. Inside she pointed to a waste bin and I dropped the wad into it.

'I'm not as green as you think,' she said. 'I was in a squad that raided a backyard abortionist and I coped but it was a while ago. All that just sort of reminded me . . .'

I arranged the burglary equipment on the coffee table. 'Got anything to drink?'

It was a couple of hours later and in her bed that we got around to talking about the night's results.

'If O'Malley has stashed Ronny somewhere to put pressure on Barry, he might not mean him actual harm,' Bron said.

'At least not immediately. But who exactly is O'Malley working for and why do they want to put pressure on Barry?'

'I get the feeling there's some sort of power play going on between all the people involved in this.'

'All the people being . . . ?'

'If I knew that . . . But they all seem to want to use Ronald to get at Bartlett . . . okay, okay, I know that's what we were doing too, but we wouldn't have killed anybody to do it.'

'You wouldn't, maybe, but what about your colleagues?'

Lying naked that close together I could almost feel her brain cogs meshing . . . evaluating . . . wondering.

'It'd help if I knew more about your investigation,' I said. 'Some details, facts and figures.'

She let out a sigh. 'I knew this was coming. How would it help?'

'When there's a conspiracy it has a sort of structure, in my experience. There are angles and people who fit into those angles. And you probe for the weak spots. You obviously thought Barry was a weak spot. CEO of what? A property development firm with transport interests, possibly connected to an oil scam. How about Sir Keith? Big in mining, wasn't he?'

'I don't know much about him. Bartlett was the focus. I want to trust you, Cliff.'

The best thing to do when someone says they want to trust you is to shut up. They will or they won't. You can't help. I kept very still and in contact with her along the length of her long body. As before, we'd pulled up the covers, a sheet and a doona, and were warm and comfortable, still a little sweaty.

'It's to do with the Mogul oil refinery at Botany,' she said.

'It's supplied from our oil fields and from foreign sources. Did you know there's a lot of oil piracy going on?'

'No.'

'They keep it quiet. The cargoes are insured and there's all sorts of lurks to explain why it doesn't always get to where it's supposed to go. Fiddling the books, cover-ups of supposed leaks, falsification of capacities and purities. So large quantities of . . . undocumented . . . oil are moving around and the Mogul operation is taking in some of it. A lot in fact.'

'Fucking oil,' I said. 'It'll be good when it runs out.'

'It won't. They won't let it, even if they have to squeeze it out of Ayers Rock.'

'I think that's sandstone.'

'Whatever. The point is there's a lot of fuel going in and out of the Mogul refinery that isn't properly monitored and it's worth millions. It's going somewhere and the government wants to know where and who's benefiting.'

I thought about it. Developments involving demolition and construction, and interstate trucking were operations that used a lot of fuel. So did mining. If BBE and Mountjoy's mining concerns were getting fuel free or at a substantial discount, they'd have a considerable advantage over their competitors. The loss of government revenue, federal and state probably, would be heavy and the legitimate movement of fuel was hemmed in with expensive safety regulations. Rogue operations wouldn't observe these and that placed the public at risk.

'Why don't the Federal Police just arrest a few people at Mogul and pull in Barry and squeeze them?'

'Mogul is a joint US and Singapore outfit and it already pays a lot of tax on its legitimate operation and employs hundreds of people, many of them in vulnerable electorates—state and federal. Get it wrong and that's a lot of powerful interests offended and we haven't got enough evidence to get it right.'

'The tax office, auditors . . .'

'Working on it, okay? But we need live, talking players, insiders with something to lose.'

'It sounds too big for Barry. I can see why he's not completely comfortable with it.'

'Maybe that's why he welcomed the arrival of the long-lost son. Someone to share the burden.'

'Hence your deployment.' I thought for a moment and then realised. 'You were going to try to turn Barry into an informer, weren't you? It's the only thing that makes sense. You thought you could get to him through Ronny, if all else failed.'

She slid out of the bed, grabbed an oversized sweater from the clothes rack and pulled it on. 'You'd better get going,' she said. 'The watchers get watched.' She didn't confirm or deny what I'd said. 'I'm going to have to come up with something on Ronald or they'll move me sideways to work on the paper trail.'

I located my clothes on the floor at the foot of the bed and dressed. 'So it wouldn't have helped much to say you knew

Ronny isn't Barry's son and you couldn't say how you learned that, anyway.'

'Right.'

'And you can't reveal that you missed where he was being kept by something like . . . half an hour.'

'Right again. Thanks a lot.'

She stood rubbing at her ruffled hair, the sloppy sweater reaching just past her crotch, leaving her taut hurdler thighs and smooth lower legs exposed. I had to look away. I wanted her again and it wasn't the time. I had to give her something. Without really thinking what I was saying, I said, 'You could tell them that you've learned Ronny was a good boxer and might have gone off with a trainer to some boxing camp in the bush.'

She stopped her search for knickers and looked at me. 'Do they have such things? I know bugger-all about boxing.'

'They do.'

'Didn't you say O'Malley was a boxer?'

I zipped up my fly and sat on the end of the bed with one sock in my hand. 'Jesus, Bron, that might just be it.'

'It! Who cares about *it*? The question is where. You've got an idea you're not going to tell me about. Fuck you!'

'It's the vaguest of possibilities and I'll keep you informed if it comes to anything, I promise. You could tell your people you've lined up an interview with Barry Bartlett. I'll arrange it. Would that keep them sweet?'

'Temporarily.'

That eased the tension and I left with us both wanting to trust each other but not sure how far we could.

In the morning I rang the hospital and was told I could visit at any time.

The morning paper carried a report on the discovery of a dead man in a house in Randwick and conveyed the police request for any member of the public, etcetera, etcetera . . . There was also a notice saying that Sir Keith's funeral would be on Tuesday at Waverley, with an archive photo of him and Lady Betty in happier times.

I showed the photos to Barry when I arrived at the hospital. He was depressed and hadn't bothered with the papers.

'I'll send a wreath,' he said. 'No Ronny?'

'Not yet, but the signs are that Des O'Malley is looking after him. I suspect it's not in your interest.'

Barry's private room was like a bedroom in a house owned by someone for whom money didn't matter. Everything, the bed, the fittings—TV, video player, phone and fax—the lighting, the view, were just as you would want them. You'd try to get better in a place like that just to enjoy it. I had a comfortable chair to sit in and Barry told me I only had to ask and I could get coffee or tea.

I gave him a sketch of what Bron had told me about the

fuel operation. He held the newspaper, staring at the photos, and didn't interrupt me.

'You've been busy,' he said when I finished. 'But it sounds as if you've been investigating my fucking business more than looking for my kid.'

'It's all linked up, Barry. Someone wants to use Ronny to get some hold over you. Who would that be, and why?'

He shook his head. The weight loss had continued, probably a good thing, but his neck was beginning to look scraggy and his eyes were deeply sunk. 'I got in over my head financially and Keith Mountjoy helped to bail me out, but there was a price.'

'Involvement in the oil scam?'

He nodded. 'I went along with it, I admit. Shit, the edge it gave me. But it started to get pricey. It took a lot of money to keep the right people sweet. Keith started to feel the pinch and we . . .'

'Wanted out?'

'Not exactly. Well, yes. We thought to sell our interest. We had some potential buyers at that drinks bash.'

'Jesus, Barry, you're in bed with Americans and Singaporeans. You don't come out on top against people like that.'

He crumpled the paper in his big, liver-spotted hands. 'I know. Why do you think my fucking blood pressure was through the roof? Keith and I were trying to work out how to shift the businesses most involved in the oil lurks and consolidate them. We were ready to cut our losses if we could do that.'

'Who was your biggest problem? Did you even know?'

'We knew all right. It was Keith's fucking wife.'

19

Barry said Mountjoy's wife was from Singapore. Educated in America, she was rich and ruthless. She'd rescued Sir Keith when one of his schemes had gone awry and fancied being Lady Mountjoy and running things.

'She bought Keith lock, stock and barrel and she got him involved in the oil rip-off. But he couldn't keep his dick in his pants and they don't get along.'

'Bad enough to have him knocked off?'

He shrugged and winced as one of the tubes running out of him snagged. 'Who knows? She's a monster.'

'And if she knew he was trying to extricate himself from the oil thing . . . ?'

'I hate to think.'

'The cops'll look at her very closely for Sir Keith's killing.'

'Good luck. She's so rich she could put herself seven steps away. You know how it works.'

'The kids didn't look Asian.'

'Earlier marriage for Keith. Accidental death, the first wife. I wouldn't be surprised if the dragon lady arranged it. Probably taught her how to go about it at Harvard, where she got her fucking MBA. So the cops are breathing down my neck, are they?'

'Yeah, but apparently they're struggling. You could . . .'

'Not a chance. You know me. Plus I've got lawyers. They can string these things out for years and I dunno how many years I've got. But I'd like to hang on to a few things for Ronny's sake. You've got to find him for me, Cliff.'

'Did you know this Titch guy?'

'Yeah, Titch Baum, he was a boxer, flyweight, pretty good but there was no money in it. Jockey for a while but he got rubbed out for something.'

More boxers, I thought. 'Did Des O'Malley go to a training camp somewhere?'

'Des? That bugger never trained. Anyway, I didn't manage him.'

'No but you managed Sione Levuka, that Fijian who fought Des in the elimination bout for the Pan-Pacific title. And I know you—you'd have found out all you could about O'Malley's preparation.'

'Yeah, you're right. It was a Mickey Mouse title but a stepping stone for Sione and Des took it seriously. He *did* train for that one. I think his people booked in at a place down at Helensburgh.'

'A farm?'

'Yeah. Jackson's farm or Johnson's or something. It's still going—trains footballers and cricketers and those mad buggers who jump off cliffs down there.'

'Hang-gliders.'

'Right. I remember hearing that Des groused about being so far from a pub. Wise choice by his people. Des was a terrible boozer in those days. Didn't do any good. Sione knocked him cold in the fifth and Des took a bad beating for a few rounds before that. He was too game for his own good. That's when Des went on the skids. I felt a bit guilty about it.'

'Why?'

He stared at the window as if it were a screen and he could see his past life playing on its dark surface. 'You know how the business works. I pressured Des's people into taking the fight. Levuka needed work to get him ready for bigger things. Des was really no match for him. That's why I took Des on later when he was in hock to the bookies and the loan sharks. I helped him get clear.'

'You're all heart, Barry.'

'Fuck you, too. Come to think of it, I believe Des mentioned that Helensburgh place once or twice after I employed him. Took women there, I suppose. You think he might've taken Ronny there?'

'It's a thought.'

He was tired now and his eyes closed and he seemed to be reprising our conversation. 'I'm not the worst,' he mumbled.

It was something I'd said myself about him and it was true. I told him I'd keep working and would let him know if I needed more money.

'Better hurry,' he said. 'While I've still got some.'

After I left I remembered that I'd told Bron I'd arrange for her to talk to Barry and I hadn't done it. Wouldn't help things between us, but tit for tat—I was sure she hadn't told me everything that was going on at her end.

I phoned Sally Brewer and asked her what she knew about a training place at Helensburgh. She had more up-to-date information than Barry.

'Jackson's Farm,' she said. 'I hear it closed down last year.'

'Why?'

'Money, why else? Same as me having to take in a partner.'

'Did you ever go there, Sal?'

'Yeah, once, to look it over. It was all right—nice old farmhouse with an accommodation wing built on. Big barn converted into a gym, swimming pool, spa and sauna. Plenty of hills to run up and down. I'd have liked to put a couple of my boys there but I couldn't afford it, too pricey. How's Barry, and how's that Ronny doing?'

I told her Barry was out of the woods and that Ronny

was okay. I asked her where Jackson's Farm was and she gave me rough directions. I put the phone down, hauled out the office folder of maps I'd collected over the years and checked the one that covered the Illawarra and Helensburgh to refresh my fading memory of the place. A dirt road named Jackson's Track snaked west into the hills. It was a long shot but I had no other leads. There was the question of Bron. The phone rang and I wondered what I should say if it was her.

'Hardy.'

'Bruce O'Connor, Hardy.'

'Detective-Sergeant, are you making progress with the Mountjoy murder?'

'I've got used to your bullshit, Hardy. I know you know more about this than you're letting on. Did you hear there was a killing in Randwick?'

My fingers tightened around the receiver. I couldn't see how the police could make any connection to me except one—through Bronwen. It was hit-and-hope time, as the golfers say.

'Saw something about it. What's it to do with me?'

I waited. Some cops are good actors, able to play teasing games with information they have or haven't got, but not this one.

'I was hoping you might tell me.'

'No idea,' I said.

'Just thought I'd ask.' He hung up.

No question that they were digging and probing in all directions and there was no telling what they might stumble on. It resolved my indecision—good time to get out of Sydney for a spell and no time to involve Bronwen.

20

Rural properties are not my favourite places. I don't mind a good sugar plantation you can admire at a safe distance from the snakes or a nice orchard where you can pick a fresh apple, but cattle farms are the worst. They smell of cow shit, which you're likely to get on your shoes, and there are too many things to trip over. My rule is: pack boots and old clothes, a slicker and a towel, because farmers pray for rain and it usually comes when you least want it. In spring in the Illawarra rain was a certainty. And, depressingly, I'd heard on the radio that it had been raining heavily there for days.

I'd been down to the Illawarra many times, usually on business, sometimes for pleasure, but I was more familiar with the coast than the escarpment and the hinterland. I'd been to Helensburgh once to a party with a girlfriend and once to give someone a bad time at a golf driving range. The party was fun, dealing with an angry man with a supply of metal clubs wasn't and I still had a scar as a memento.

I loaded the car with the things I'd need, like the clothes and a powerful torch, and things I'd want, like a bottle of scotch. The .38 was somewhere in between want and need.

I took the Princes Highway under a cloudy sky to Waterfall, where I filled the tank and then went on for a short distance before turning off at the Helensburgh sign. The rainstorm hit just then and wind gusts rocked the car. Another fifteen minutes of wet driving took me to the town with its overflowing gutters and trees being shrapnelled by the rain, and I stopped for coffee. I spread the map out on the table and aroused the interest of the kid working in the coffee shop.

'Where're you headed?' he asked as he put the coffee mug down.

I pointed to Jackson's Track.

He shook his head. 'Is that your Falcon out there?'

I nodded.

'Never make it. The track's sure to be cut by run-offs and overflows. It's been pissing down the last few days. You'd need a bloody good four-wheel-drive.'

'Thanks.'

He nodded and went back behind the counter. I drank the coffee, which was pretty good, and looked out the window at the pelting rain. *I'm a summer guy*, I thought. *Sand and surf. What am I doing down here in Noah's fucking flood?*

'Anywhere I can hire one?'

'You're keen.' He pointed to a noticeboard beside the register. It was festooned with business cards, one for a firm hiring out earth-moving equipment, trucks and 4WDs.

He gave me the directions and I left him a substantial tip. Outside, the rain had eased off but the gutters were still flowing fast. People dashed between awnings with their umbrellas and the traffic was crawling, mindful of potholes and the occasional blocked drain sending a sheet of water across the road.

Twenty minutes later I was in possession of a Nissan Patrol with my gear safely packed in and the Falcon parked in the hire firm's yard. The wipers, always a bit iffy in the old Falcon, worked a treat and I could feel the grip of new tyres. Back window wipers were a plus. The Nissan handled well, the power steering not too light, not too heavy. Three turns off the main street and I was at the beginning of Jackson's Track, which began life as an adequately drained gravel road.

Neither the draining nor the gravel persisted. After a few kilometres the track lived up to its name as it became a narrow dirt stretch, potholed and sticky with the promised runnels and wash-outs starting to occur as it wound its way steadily upwards. The bush was thick on both sides, obscuring the track ahead at the bends. The driving required my full concentration; a vehicle coming the other way would present a serious challenge, under the conditions. The stability of the track's edges was problematical.

For all that I enjoyed the Nissan's capacity to cope with the surface, the axle-deep washes and the steady rain, mud splashed up onto the bonnet and body of the car turned the car more brown than its original white. Did my contract oblige me to wash it before returning it? I couldn't remember.

After the first few kilometres there were no turn-offs and it was clear that Jackson's Track was a dedicated route to Jackson's Farm. The track flattened out about the same time as the rain eased and the bush thinned out. The mud lay thicker but there were fewer sheets of falling water and more puddles. The tall, swaying trees had kept the light down on the drive but it grew brighter as they receded and there were paddocks on either side and an occasional cattle grid made itself felt under the mud and washed-along debris.

The rain had eased to a drizzle and stopped as I rounded a gentle bend. Fifty yards ahead I saw a chest-high metal gate stretched across the track and a sign that read:

JACKSON'S FARM

PRIVATE PROPERTY

TRESPASSERS PROSECUTED

No phone number or way to make contact. The gate was set into two steel posts and fastened with a thick chain and padlock. A rusty padlock can be tricky but one in good condition is, literally, easy pickings if you have the tools.

THAT EMPTY FEELING

I dealt with the lock in a minute or two and pushed the heavy gate open.

There are three rules for approaching unchecked-upon country premises: be prepared for unfriendly dogs, when parking turn your vehicle back the way you came, and leave the gate open. The last violates country practice from Cape York to Wilsons Promontory but I wasn't about to ignore it. Any livestock would have to take its chances.

I pinned the gate open with a stick pushed deep into the mud and drove slowly up to a farmhouse just visible around a wide, curving, rain-washed concrete strip.

21

I took the .38 from the glove-box and put it in my pocket, parked and got out of the car. The parking area was well laid and maintained gravel but the heavy rain had created puddles. I stepped straight into one, but with solid hiking boots on my feet I didn't care. The afternoon air was cold at this elevation; smoke drifted up from the chimney of the main house—a large, traditional, double-fronted structure with a wide bullnose veranda in front and down the west side. A two-storey add-on was visible at the back on the east side.

I stood at the bottom of the three steps leading to the veranda to see if my arrival had sparked any activity. The steps were built of sandstone blocks and railway sleepers, deeply scuffed by generations of boots. No sounds, no movement. I went up the steps and knocked at the door. The last thing I expected to hear was the click of high heels on a hardwood floor. The door opened and a young woman stood there, cigarette in hand and attitude in place. She was wearing the same kind of Arsenal cap and scarf I'd seen Ronny wearing when we left the gym for the pub.

'Who the fuck are you?' she said.

I told her to shut up and backed up the order by taking out the pistol. I grabbed her by the arm and pushed her in front of me down the passage.

'That fuckin' hurts,' she squealed.

'It'll hurt more if you don't behave. Where's Ronny?'

She pointed to a door a little further down the passage. I sucked in a breath: not mission accomplished, but progress made. I tightened my grip on her skinny arm.

'Who else is here? And where's Des?'

'No one else. Des's g-gone huntin'.'

'In the rain?'

'Rain stopped ten minutes ago.'

True enough. I released her arm, pushed her hard against the wall and gave her a good look at the gun before I put it away.

'I don't want to hurt you but I will if I have to. Go into the living room, sit down, keep smoking and keep quiet and you'll be okay. Got it?'

She nodded and tottered away, puffing furiously on her cigarette and not looking back. Although it was cool in the house, all she wore was a skimpy black lacy bra, an unbuttoned white satin blouse and black satin tights. Stiletto heels. The scarf provided a bit of warmth without compromising the display. She wasn't there to do the cooking and cleaning.

I eased open the door she'd indicated. The smell—a pungent blend of booze, sweat, massage oil and sperm—hit me before the physical details of the room. Ronny, only his head, upper chest and shoulders visible above a tartan blanket, lay in the middle of a three-quarter bed. Trousers, shirts, a sweater and underwear lay scattered on the carpeted floor. A couple of bottles and glasses sat on a card table in a corner of the room. I went in and saw a handbasin in a corner with two pill bottles and a plastic syringe on it.

Ronny was asleep. His hair was lank and his face pale, but his breathing was even and fairly deep. The upper part of his chest and his shoulders were covered with scratches and love bites. He had a few days' stubble and some spittle at the edges of his mouth. When I tried to rouse him he snored and threw one tattooed arm out from under the blanket, but otherwise didn't respond. Champagne and scotch on the card table; Rohypnol and something I couldn't identify on the washbasin.

I left the room and opened the next door. An overnight bag spilling women's clothes lay on the floor. I grabbed the fluffy white coat hanging on the back of the door and went down the passage. The woman, still smoking, was sitting hunched near a dying fire. She looked up at me with wide frightened eyes that weren't quite focused.

'Put some logs on,' I said.

She held up hands with nails like talons, painted bright red.

Hence the scratches, I thought.

I draped the coat over her shoulders, took the poker and prodded at the embers and put some kindling and a couple of light logs on the fire. The kindling caught and I held my cold hands out to the warmth. She threw her cigarette into the fire and shrugged the coat around her.

'Comfy?' I said.

'I'm okay.'

'What's your name?'

'Eve.'

'Very nice. Easy to remember and spell—same way backwards and forwards. So what's the deal here, Evie?'

She waved at a table in the middle of the room. 'Will you get me a fag?'

'When I get some information.'

'Are you a cop?'

I showed her the licence. 'Private enquiries; could be better than the cops, could be worse. Up to you.'

'I haven't done anything.'

'A man has been abducted and held under restraint. Drugs have been used. Those are serious crimes, worse than your pick-ups for soliciting.'

Eve was in her middle twenties and, at a guess, had ten years of bad experience with men and drugs and struggling to stay alive behind her. As she picked at the fraying polish on her nails and rubbed at the nicotine stains on the fingers of her right hand I could see her working out how much to play me, just another man out to do her harm.

'Des is an old friend,' she said.

Read client, I thought. 'Yes?'

'He comes to me and he says he's got this young bloke who needs to lie low for a while but he needs, like, some encouragement to get out of Sydney and stay out. I didn't know nothing about the drugs. When I first met him I just thought he was pissed. Well, I've had some experience dealing with drunks and that.'

'I can imagine. Did Des say why he needed to go bush?'

That was the first serious question she'd faced. How much she knew led to how much this was her responsibility. She hesitated and stared out the nearest window. I could read her mind.

'The sun's shining, love,' I said. 'After being cooped up in the rain for days, Des'll be happy to be out and about. Especially if he's got a toy to play with. If I know Des, he'll have taken a bottle with him and he'll shoot at anything that moves, or doesn't. He could be away the rest of the day.'

She nodded. 'He didn't say much at first but then he got a phone call and he started Ronny on the Roies and the pethidine. He reckoned he had to keep him for longer than he thought.'

'Why?'

'He said some people wanted to use Ronny to get at his father somehow, but it had all gone wrong. That's all I know.'

It wasn't, I could tell, but how to get more out of her? 'How much is Des paying you?'

She shrugged. 'A grand.'

'Has he paid you yet?'

'Bits.'

'I can guarantee you two thousand bucks, no questions asked, if you tell me what else you know.'

'How can you guarantee that much?'

'I'm working for Ronny's father. He's very rich. He'll be grateful to get Ronny back and he doesn't need to know you fucked and drugged him into a coma.'

'A coma?'

'What it looks like to me. He's not good. I have to get him to a hospital pretty quickly after I talk to Des.'

'Give me a fag.'

I got the Winfields from the assortment of things on the table and handed the packet to her with her lighter. She lit up, sucked the smoke deep and blew a long plume into the fire that was now burning brightly.

'Couple of nights ago, when Ronny was well and truly out, Des and me had a fuck. He was pretty pissed and sounding off about this bastard he reckoned had found them and how his mate Titch had copped it.'

'Copped it how?'

'Dead. Shit, I never expected to get into this fuckin' mess.

It was just a job, a cushy fuckin' job. I guess there's no such thing.'

'Right. Last question. Who's Des working for?'

She'd smoked half of the cigarette already. 'I have no fuckin' idea.'

'For whoever it was wanting to use Ronny against his dad?'

'I suppose, but I dunno.'

I sat back and thought about it while she continued smoking. I'd been puzzled by the attempt to take Ronny away from Des in Randwick. Now it was clearer: perhaps Des had tried to make his own private deal and it had gone sour.

I said, 'How did you get here?'

'Land Rover.'

'Where is it?'

'In a garage at the back.'

'Where're the keys?'

She pointed to the mess on the table.

'Can you drive?'

'Yeah. Lost my licence, but.'

'Doesn't matter. Pack up your stuff. You're leaving.'

I took a hundred dollars from my wallet and handed it to her. 'This is to get you on your way. You give me a number where I can get in touch with you to pay you the two grand.'

Life and hope returned. She jumped up, located a handbag among the mess and rooted through it. She found a pencil and scribbled a number on a scrap of torn newspaper.

'What about Des?'

'I'll take care of Des. He won't bother you.'

She scurried away and returned with her overnight bag packed. She'd put on tight jeans and a sweater and exchanged her stilettos for solid-heeled boots. I picked up the keys to the Land Rover and we went through the kitchen and back sunroom to the yard and a two-car garage with unlocked sliding doors. I handed her the keys.

'What sort of a gun has he got?'

'How d'you mean?'

'Shotgun or rifle?'

'Search me. Perhaps a shotgun?'

'Watch yourself on that track down, it's bloody tricky.'

'You're a good bloke, whoever the fuck you are.'

'No, I'm not,' I said. 'Just practical.'

The Land Rover started at a touch; she backed it out efficiently, turned, waved and drove off. I followed her around the house and watched her disappear down Jackson's Track. Then I went back inside and waited for Des O'Malley, former contender for the Pan-Pacific middleweight title.

22

The land at the back of the house sloped gently upward and spread out to the north and the south. I made periodic trips inside to check on Ronny, have a piss, make a sandwich and drink a can of beer from the slab of Toohey's Des had in the fridge. But I was never away from my lookout post for more than five minutes. After about two hours I saw him coming over the hill down towards the house. He had the rifle or shotgun across his shoulders at the back, secured by his crossed arms, like Steve McQueen in *Nevada Smith*. *Good*, I thought. *It takes quite a while to get from that self-satisfied macho pose into a shooting position.*

I stood behind a half-folded-back screen that was designed to give some shade on the open back porch until Des was safely in pistol range. I stepped out and down with the .38 pointed squarely at his broad chest.

'Gidday, Des. Don't move a muscle. I don't see any bunnies. Too quick for you, were they?'

He stood with his mouth hanging open. He was wearing a flannie over a T-shirt, mud-splashed jeans and rubber boots. No hat; the bald head gleamed in the afternoon light.

'Hardy.'

'Right, locked and loaded. Unship the weapon, Des, and let it drop easy.'

'It's unloaded.'

'So you say. Again, let it go easy, no throwing.'

He released what I could now see was a shotgun and let it drop onto the wet, foot-trodden grass.

'Where's the slut?'

'Gone, in the Land Rover.'

'The kid?'

'In my care.'

He took a flask from the pocket in his jeans and had a long swig. 'Who're you working for, Hardy?'

'Funny, that's exactly what I was just going to ask you.'

'Fuck you.'

He threw the flask at me with a quickness I wouldn't have credited him with. I dodged and it missed but it gave him time to come bullocking towards me, roaring, shouting and getting too close, too quickly, for me to bring the gun back to bear on him. He made a battering ram of his head and hunched body and knocked me sideways so that I reached at a post for support and lost my grip on the gun. It went spinning away.

I regained my balance in time to avoid his first wild swing. I circled away as he went into the Mike Tyson-style crouch he'd adopted in his ill-starred ring career.

'I've been looking forward to this, Hardy.'

The trouble with fighting ex-professional boxers is that they know all the tricks—the quick moves, then deceptively slow ones, the feints, the counters to various punches. They learn them over hours in the gym and they employ them under pressure when it comes to the real thing. They remain ingrained even for an overweight, over-the-hill pug like Des O'Malley.

We moved around each other on the slushy ground without doing much damage. I was lighter and quicker, with better wind, but he knew a trick or two I didn't and he landed a couple of heavy punches that stung, one high on my right cheekbone and one to the right shoulder. Another shot like that to my shoulder and I'd lose some feeling in the arm, and that could be fatal.

The only advantage I had was better footing. He was clumsy in his wellies and aware of it, so he kept his foot movements short and precise. He caught me again with a left rip to the side that had me backing away and I had to take a chance. I gasped as though I was really hurt, dropped my hands and sagged. He gave a grunt of triumph, abandoned caution and almost rushed in. I'd chosen the spot and his feet went from under him on the particularly greasy patch of ground. He fought for balance but I was set, ready and desperate. I landed a straight right with all my weight behind it below the ear on the hinge of his jaw. His neck twisted violently. I heard a click and his yelp of pain and alarm but by then I had retrieved the pistol and I clubbed him hard with its butt on the right temple. He went down like an animal shot with an anaesthetic dart.

I stood over him, panting and hoping I hadn't broken his neck. Unlikely; it was well padded with muscle and fat. I dragged him through the mud, hoisted him up on the porch and propped him against the wall of the house. I used my Swiss army knife to cut lengths from a roll of garden twine I'd found in the house and tied his hands in front of him and his feet at the ankles. I tilted him unresistingly sideways and took his wallet from his hip pocket.

It was gratifying to see that one of my punches had split his lower lip. I went inside, soaked a tea towel and took two cans from the slab. Back on the porch, Des was stirring. He looked at me with eyes bulging and blinking at the same time.

'You've broke my fuckin' neck.'

'Don't think so. Give it a wobble, up and down and side to side.'

Despite himself he did as I said and made the movements without trouble although it clearly hurt him.

'There you are. You're all right. Nasty cut lip but you were game enough in your day, Des. You'd have been able to go a few more rounds.'

'I'll kill you, Hardy.'

'Don't think so. You had your chance.'

I gave him the tea towel and took it away as soon as he'd wiped the blood from his face. Then I cracked the cans and gave him one.

'Time for a little talk, Des, and please don't say fuck you again. At least come up with something more original.'

He set himself to say it again but thought better of it and clamped his mouth shut. That hurt his lip and he yelped and licked at the split. He drank as best he could with the side of his mouth.

'I'll help you get started,' I said. 'Someone paid you to take Ronny and you worked out who'd hired them. You tried to make your own deal for more money but it went to shit and somehow Titch got shanked. You've burnt your boats with Barry, that's for sure, and you've lost Ronny. What've you got to lose by telling me who you were working for and why?'

He shook his head and drank more beer.

'Had to be someone planning to use Ronny as a tool against his dad. I can tell you this, the Federal Police had the same idea but it didn't quite work out.'

His eyes widened in surprise but he stayed silent.

'It's big stuff, Des. Too big for you. Probably too big for me. Nothing to say? Okay, let's do a bit of detecting.'

I opened his wallet and went through the contents—driver's licence, RSL membership card, bank keycard, sixty-nine dollars, a card for Paddington Pussies, two lottery tickets, cards for various businesses like a motor mechanic and a laundromat, and a stiff white one for Ratan Mining International with an address in Singapore. CEO Lady Betty Lee Mountjoy.

I held the card up for O'Malley. 'That who you're working for?'

'She'll cut your heart out,' he said. I took that as confirmation—but who was the middleman he'd tried to double cross?

I pulled O'Malley upright and shoved him across to where I could dump him in a plastic chair. I twisted about a dozen turns of the twine around him so he was anchored to the chair and only able to move his arms from the elbows. He could just get to the beer can he was clutching to his mouth.

I went into the house and cut the phone cord. With great difficulty I fitted Ronny into some clothes and shoes. He had deep purple and yellow bruises on his ribs on both sides and movement hurt him, even though the drugs had dulled him down. Eve had left the cap and the scarf; I jammed the cap on his head and wound the scarf around his neck. He groaned as I put him in a fireman's lift and carried him out to the Nissan. I arranged him in the back seat and strapped him in with my bundled-up anorak as a pillow. He muttered and then he snored. He smelled terrible. I turned the engine on and left it running.

'I'm off, Des,' I said, 'me and Ronny.'

He showed fear for the first time. 'You goin' to leave me here to fuckin' die?'

'No.'

I gave him a very blunt kitchen knife I'd found in a drawer. 'You can cut yourself loose with this. It'll take a while, but you can do it. Don't drop the knife, mind.'

'You say the chick took the car?'

'That's right. Looked like she could handle it, too.'

'How am I going to get out of here?'

I handed him the knife. 'Walk. But look at it this way— it's mostly downhill.'

On the way out I picked up Des's shottie, checked that it wasn't loaded and hurled it as far as I could into the bush.

23

I took it quietly down the track, stopping from time to time to make sure Ronny was okay. The driving was easier now that the rain had stopped. The guy in the hire place was surprised to see me back so soon but not surprised at the state of the vehicle.

'You're up for the petrol and the wash, mate. It'll come out of your deposit.'

I told him that was fine and while he went off to do the paperwork I shifted Ronny and my gear to the Falcon, I put him on the back seat with his head cushioned as before and a blanket over him. He was twitching a bit but still fast asleep. I settled up and drove back to the main street and stopped at the first telephone box I found to ring Bronwen.

'Bron, it's Cliff.'

Coolly, 'Nice to hear from you.'

'I've got Ronny.'

'*What?*'

'I've got him. Can you be at my place in an hour and a half? I need some help.'

'Is he all right?'

'Not really.'

'I'll be there. Is there anything else?'

'No, I'll explain everything when I see you.'

'You better.'

She hung up and I got on my way. I mulled over her response as I drove. It was reasonable that she'd be annoyed at my absence and silence but not that she should adopt that high moral tone. Or maybe it was. In the strange relationship we had forming, anything was possible. I drove with great care, not only out of consideration for my passenger but because I had two bottles of prescription medicine, a vial of an analgesic drug and a half-loaded plastic syringe in my pocket.

I saw Bron's Audi as soon as I turned into my street. She got out and came quickly towards me. She was wearing her business gear and looking efficient. Ronny was stirring and she helped me get him from the car, into the house and up the stairs to the spare room. We stripped him off and washed him down, paying particular attention to places where he'd vomited on himself and being gentle with the bruises. He protested mildly and incoherently but didn't resist.

'At least he didn't shit himself,' Bron said.

'Probably the reverse problem. The sorts of drugs he's had pumped into him cause constipation.'

'Know a bit about it, do you?'

'At second hand.'

Bron held his head while I helped him to sip some water. After that he went back to sleep.

'Aren't you supposed to walk them up and down?' Bron said.

But I was already on the phone to my doctor, Ian Sangster. I described the symptoms and named the two drugs I knew he'd taken.

'That's a pretty heavy load. Can someone keep an eye on him until I get there in an hour or so? I take it you don't want to take him to a hospital.'

'Not unless I have to, but I'll let that be your decision.'

'Thanks a lot, I love compromising my medical ethics for you.'

'Thanks, Ian. You know your life would be duller without me.'

I finished the call. Bron was sitting beside Ronny's pale, bewhiskered head at the top of the bed and I was in the hallway checking my answering machine for messages. There weren't any. Suddenly, she was standing beside me and pulling me to my feet.

'Life certainly isn't dull around you,' she said.

She kissed me and pulled me close. She touched my bruised cheekbone and looked at my eye that by then would have been showing some damage.

'Bad fight?'

'Not when you win.'

'I was angry when you took off without telling me anything.'

I held on to her, enjoying the softness, the hardness and the warmth. 'Love, it was a matter of a drive up a muddy track, a shotgun and a bare-knuckle stoush. You . . .'

Ever the professional, she eased back. 'A shotgun? That's what killed Sir Keith Mountjoy.'

I shook my head. 'That was a shortened shottie, this was the full monty.'

'You're infuriating.'

'I know. Look, what I need is a strong coffee with a decent belt of whisky in it and something to eat. Then we can sit down until Ian comes and I can tell you all about it.'

'All? Knowing you, I doubt it.'

She was right. There were quite a few things to sort out between us before I could tell her everything.

Ian arrived and gave Ronny a thorough examination. I showed him the drugs and told him there'd been a lot of alcohol as well.

'Over how long?' he asked.

'Not long, about four days.'

'Long enough. His life's not in danger. Those bruises are bad but his ribs aren't broken, though they might be cracked.

Whoever did that knew what he was doing. Your guy's young and very fit, but he's going to need some R and R. There's a place in Erskineville I could get him into. Very expensive.'

'Not a problem. Barry Bartlett'll pay.'

This conversation went on outside the spare room. Ronny was drowsily awake through the examination but not taking any interest in what was happening to him. Bron was in with him and I could hear encouraging murmurs from her. Ian made a couple of calls. I phoned the hospital, asked for Barry and was told he was attending a session on diet and nutrition. Had to smile at that. I left a message that Ronny was safe and that I would be calling on him that evening.

Bron and I drove Ronny to the Darnley Rest and Rehabilitation Centre near the Erskineville Oval park. Ian had provided the technical data and we checked him in, leaving my details and Barry's. Ronny still showed almost no interest in the proceedings but offered us a smile and a nod before he was wheelchaired away.

'Who was she?' Bron asked when we got back to her car.

'Who was who?'

'The woman who was with him. Think I don't know what a love bite looks like? And those scratches, Jesus!'

'A hooker, name of Eve, but probably not.'

'And how did you deal with her? Charm?'

'Money. Barry's going to have to pay her two thousand. I have to tell him what's happened and to save me doing it twice you'd better come along.'

'And on the way you'll work out how much to tell us.'

I nodded. 'You've got it.'

'How will you explain me?'

'I'm working on it.'

Barry was looking a lot better when we got to him. He'd shaved or been shaved and was scrubbed up. He wore white silk pyjamas and had lost some of the haggard look. I introduced Bron as my assistant who'd helped me to find Ronny.

'You look years younger,' I said.

'I feel okay, might make a play for Ms Marr here. Tell me about the boy.'

I told him how the Helensburgh suggestion had worked out and how O'Malley and the prostitute had kept him under control. I touched the black eye.

'I went one-on-one with Des and got lucky. I had to buy off the girl. You owe her two grand.'

Barry waved that away. 'He's all right, then?'

I explained how my doctor had examined Ronny and how Bron and I had taken him to the rest home. 'More money, I'm afraid, Barry.'

'That's all right. It's my fault he got into this shit.' He nodded at Bron. 'Thanks.'

Bron knew most of this but controlled her impatience. She sat quietly, appraising the man who was one of her main targets.

'Okay,' Barry said. 'Why and who?'

'To get some sort of hold on you, obviously. Who's behind it I still don't know, but I've got a lead.'

Out of the corner of my eye I saw Bron react negatively to my first statement and more positively to the second. I told them that I'd left Eve in charge of the 4WD that had taken the three of them to the farm.

'My guess is she'll hang on to it. I've got the licence number and I want to take a look at it for the sort of stuff that accumulates in cars. It's not Des's kind of vehicle. With luck, I should be able to trace it to whoever . . . financed him.'

Barry nodded enthusiastically and Bron did the same a little less happily.

'*Cherchez la femme*,' Bron said. 'That's you all over, Cliff.'

Barry looked puzzled.

'It's okay,' I said. 'I've got a contact number for the girl. I'm going to need the two thousand, though.'

'I'll get on it,' Barry said, pointing to his phone. 'Should be able to have it couriered to you by tomorrow morning. That do?'

'Yeah, then we can . . .'

I'd turned to Bron to include her in this and she looked worried.

'What?' I said.

'Cliff, I need a private word. Sorry, Mr Bartlett.'

'Barry.'

'Barry. Sorry. Cliff?'

I gave Barry a you-know-what-they're-like shrug and followed Bron out of the room. She was rigid with anger and would have bailed me up against the wall if she'd had the height and weight.

'You're a bastard. You're hiding something to protect that fucking crook.'

'What d'you mean? You can come with me when I go to see Eve and—'

'Fuck that. I can read you. You've got something more solid you're not telling me. Let me talk to him.'

'No. It's not the right time. He won't talk to you now.'

'Okay, that's it! Partnership dissolved.' She walked away, heels clicking, skirt flicking with the roll of her angry hips.

I went back into the room. Barry made a face. 'I heard a bit. Cliff, tell me I'm wrong, but I thought I smelled cop.'

'You're not wrong,' I said. 'I'm in a tough spot, Barry. She's Federal Police, part of a task force working on your fuel scam.'

'Shit, what're you doing teaming up with her for then?'

'She helped a lot.'

'Are you fucking her?'

'I was, but probably not anymore. She knows I'm holding out on her and she'll be firmly on your case now. She might try to milk Ronny for more information but I don't think he has any. That's about all she can do.'

'You're holding out how?'

'I think I know who hired Des.'

'Who?'

I shook my head. 'This is what I mean by being in a tough spot. You're my client and I want to protect you. How deeply are you into this thing?'

'Too fucking deep. I told you, I was looking to get out of it.'

'How hard have you been along the way?'

'What d'you mean?'

'Had anyone killed?'

'Shit, no.'

'Would you rat on the others in return for immunity?'

'What others?'

'Whoever.'

'You *are* playing it close to the fucking chest.'

He stared at me. As far as I knew, and his attitude now seemed to confirm it, Barry had never been a phiz-gig although he would've had plenty of opportunities. But in the era of Neddy Smith and others, the old code of silence was breaking down.

Barry suddenly lost the glow he'd had when I arrived. He heaved a deep sigh. 'I'd die in gaol, Cliff, if I was sent up for my part in it. Don't want that, and there's Ronny to think of. Yeah, I'd talk to save my hide if you could swing it. So, who tried to grab Ronny? The Mountjoys?'

I got up from my chair, my joints cracking, my muscles aching. 'At this stage, Barry, it's better you don't know. Make it three thousand in the morning, okay?'

'Mate, I'll make it four.'

I went home to an empty house. No word from Bron, as I'd expected. I knew I'd have to negotiate with her and her colleagues at some point, but I'd need some better cards in my hand before that. I was dog-tired, went to bed early and had a deep, dreamless sleep. If there was a hair of Bronwyn's dark head on the pillow or a whiff of her body in the bed I didn't notice.

At 10.30 the next morning a courier brought a package—four thousand dollars in hundreds and fifties. I put two thousand in an envelope, a couple of hundred in my wallet and the rest into a drawer and locked it. The .38 went back into its hiding place; the muddy boots stood outside the back door waiting for a clean and the muddy trousers went into the wash. Then I rang the number Eve had given me.

'Hullo.' A male voice.

'I'd like to speak to Eve.'

'Who would?'

'Tell her I've got her money.'

I heard a series of noises—voices, a slap, footsteps . . .

'Hello, this is Eve.'

'I've got your two thousand. Do you want it?'

'Bet your life I want it. Fuck me, you kept your word.'

'Life's full of surprises, isn't it? Who answered the phone?'

'Nobody. How do I get the money?'

'I'll bring it to you. I'm hoping you've still got the Land Rover.'

'Yeah, you going to take it away?'

'No, I just want to look it over. Where are you?'

She said she still had the car and gave me an address in Petersham.

'Any trouble likely from Nobody?'

She laughed. 'Not when I tell him what you done to Des O'Malley.'

'How do you know what I did to O'Malley?'

'I hear things. Word is he got back last night and was very knocked about. He's in hospital with a cracked skull.'

'Must have tripped and fallen. By the way, does Des have a sawn-off shottie?'

'Sure he does, loves waving it about. Gave me the shits.'

I'd used the idea of learning something from the Land Rover to fob Bronwen off but I was serious about it. I knew Betty Lee Mountjoy was involved but it wouldn't hurt to get another name or two—personal or corporate. I topped up the Falcon's tank, reflecting how twenty bucks would've overflowed it a few years ago and now it fell well short of full. I supposed the stuff was dearer to get out of the ground, and there were tricky politics involved, but the oil companies and the government had seized the chance to get in for their whack on the basis of the uncertainty.

The address was for a terrace house close to the railway station. A grey, soulless street, but not too far from the attractions of the Portuguese quarter with its restaurants and take-aways. I promised myself a lunch of sardines and salad on Barry.

Eve, cigarette in hand, opened the door. She was wearing what she'd worn when she drove off yesterday. I had the envelope in my hand and she reached for it.

'Keys first,' I said, 'and where is it?'

'In the fuckin' station carpark. Will you bring the keys back?'

Had to hand it to her, she was still negotiating. 'You can do what you like with it as far as I'm concerned.'

She reached into her back pocket and handed me the keys. I gave her the envelope and she flicked through the notes with greedy fingers. 'Is it hot, the 4WD?'

'Not now,' I said. 'Could be later.'

'I fancy the Gold Coast. Plenty of action and a long way from Des.'

'Good idea,' I said. 'I'll drop the keys back through the letter slot.'

The Land Rover, sitting among rows of commuter cars, was as dirty as the Nissan had been, or even dirtier. It also sported two parking infringement notices and its radio aerial had been snapped off. Leave a vehicle in a car space overnight in the inner west and that's what you get.

I unlocked it. It smelled of cigarette smoke and the ashtray had overflowed. Eve must've smoked a whole packet on her way down Jackson's Track. I climbed in, opened the glove-box and scooped the contents out—chewing gum, an empty cigarette packet, used tissues, a dead lighter, an ATM transaction slip for a hundred dollars and a registration certificate. The vehicle was registered to Botany Security Systems. I pocketed the certificate and the ATM slip. I opened the bonnet and removed the distributor cap. If Eve had been hoping to drive it to Surfers she was going to be disappointed. It'd either sit there suffering more vandalism or be towed to the RTA holding yard. Either way suited me. I wanted to create worry about it. I kept the keys.

I rang Harry Tickener, assuming he'd be in his office on a Sunday, and asked him what he knew about Botany Security Systems. I waited while he consulted his files.

'It's a security firm which, rumour has it, lists some pretty big concerns among its clients,' Harry said.

'Such as?'

He ran off a list of names that included Ratan Mining and Mogul Resources. 'Sounds as if you're making progress. Anything for me?'

'Not yet. Could be a while.'

'Watch yourself, Cliff, those security outfits have a habit of hiring some pretty rough types.'

'How can you say that? I've been approached myself by a couple of these places over the years.'

'Like I said.'

'You reckon they're subcontracting work out?'

'I wouldn't be at all surprised.'

I rang Botany Security, hoping they operated on a seven-day week and was relieved when the phone was answered. I asked if anyone in a senior position was available to speak to.

'About what, sir?'

'A vehicle registered to you.' I read off the numberplate.

'Involved in an accident?'

'Not exactly. You give that number to someone upstairs or in a decent office. I'll hang on.'

After a long pause a different voice, with a South African or Rhodesian accent, came on the line. 'Who am I talking to?'

'I think you know.'

'And if I do?'

'You'll want to get the vehicle back and come to some arrangement with me.'

'Financial?'

'Partly.'

'What else?'

'When I have someone to talk to.'

'Okay. Where and when?'

'Jubilee Park at the bottom of Glebe Point Road this afternoon at 3.30. I know the place and its approaches like the back of my hand and I have helpers. I want one person who knows what this is about and just him, or her. It's turned a bit chilly so he or she should wear a red scarf. He or she can be armed if he wants, because I will be.'

'You can cut the gender equality crap. I'll be there.'

He hung up and I let out a long, slow breath.

A spring cold snap, deterring the Jubilee Park joggers, and the dog-walkers were keeping well away from the bay where every now and then a shark, at least in local legend, had taught Rover not to swim. I was standing by one of the giant Moreton Bay figs down near the water, taking shelter from a keen-edged wind, when a white Holden station wagon with a corporate badge on the side came slowly down the road. It made a careful U-turn at the barrier and parked pointing back the way it had come. I had to smile—a fellow professional. That might make things easier, or possibly harder.

24

The red scarf stood out against the grey day backdrop. Big bloke, cropped dark hair, buff-coloured trench coat, long, confident stride. I moved out from behind the tree and he saw me. He glanced around purely as a reflex action, not expecting to see anyone else and he didn't. His big black Oxfords crunched the crisp leaves as he came towards me. Stopped a yard away.

'You are Cliff Hardy.' With the accent it sounded more like an accusation than an identification. 'I know all about you. You've already been a bloody nuisance to me.'

'Right, and you are?'

'Richard Keppler.'

'Gidday, Dick. Glad to meet you.'

'Skip the funny business, hey? Let's get to it.' He mimed a sweeping look around. 'I don't see the Land Rover.'

I was wearing a leather jacket with deep pockets. I had the .38 in one and the keys to the Land Rover, the registration certificate and the distributor cap in the other. The pistol stayed where it was; I took the other things out.

'It's in the carpark at Petersham railway station, or possibly the RTA holding depot. I don't know.'

He shrugged. 'And what do you want?'

'It's too cold to just stand here. Let's walk.'

He agreed reluctantly and we set off towards the bridge across the canal. The park was due for an upgrade and residents were looking forward to the clearance of some industrial sites, slipways and the restoration of a wetland. Good luck.

'I think you hired Desmond O'Malley to kidnap Ronald Saunders to use him to exert influence over Barry Bartlett. This was on the orders of Betty Lee Mountjoy.' I remembered Barry saying Des had done some security work. 'In fact, I think Des has been working for you for years on the quiet. But this time I think he tried to go freelance and your thugs found him and killed Titch Baum in the process.'

'Oh? That's a lot of thinking.' He sounded bored, but I'd seen the sudden angry twitch near his eye before he turned away again.

'Yeah. I think Lady Betty was afraid Barry was going to bail out . . . or even worse, turn snitch. I have evidence.'

'Do you?'

'Yes, but I don't care about that. I've handled that situation. You also have a contract with the Mogul refinery.'

He had his hands deep in the pockets of his coat where I assumed he had a gun. But there were people around, not close but close enough to give pause. We stood on the bridge with the dirty water rushing below us. He seemed reluctant to speak.

'I'm not wired,' I said. Still keeping my hand on the pistol, I opened my jacket and let him pat me down.

'You might have it in your underpants.'

'I don't. I'll pull it out and take a piss right here if you like. This is between you and me, Dick. I've got a few things to hide, not as much as you, but we're kind of in this together.'

His pale Dutch eyes bored into me for a moment and then he nodded. I told him about the fuel scam being worked by BBE and Ratan Mining and their subsidiaries. I said someone inside the Mogul operation was arranging things at the flow end to allow the scam to work.

'I don't know anything about this,' he said.

'Maybe you don't, but you can find out and when you do, you and I'll talk to the Federal Police.'

He laughed, took his hands from his pockets and rubbed them together to warm them. 'I can't see that happening.'

'It will, because as well as evidence about your kidnapping caper, I can prove that O'Malley was contracted to kill Sir Keith Mountjoy. How would you like Botany Security to be involved in that?'

It was a colossal bluff but I'd supplied just enough information that, together with the chance to recover the

Land Rover, made him consider it. If he'd done his research on me he'd know that, while I wasn't in particularly good standing with the police, I had an important and influential contact in Frank Parker and an honourable army record.

He swung around towards the water to do his thinking and I put the hook in a bit deeper.

'The thing is, Dick, Betty Lee wasn't the only one to have the idea of using young Ronny. The federal cops set up a honey trap for him but I managed to intervene there as well. I've got the woman in question onside.'

I stiffened for a second as he dipped into his coat pocket but he took out a pipe and a tin of Uncle Pat tobacco. He filled the pipe and lit it and I was carried back years to when I was a small boy in Maroubra and my grandfather smoked Uncle Pat. I sniffed appreciatively at the rich smoke and he looked at me with an expression that was close to a smile, as if we had somehow communicated on another level.

'I'll see what I can do. I'm not sure quite what's in this for you.'

I decided to be honest with him and, to my surprise, with myself. 'I'm hoping for immunity for Barry Bartlett and I'm interested in the woman I spoke of.'

He puffed and nodded. 'Immunity sounds good. I'd need something similar myself.'

'Negotiable,' I said, and handed him the keys and the distributor cap.

Pipe in mouth, he reached inside his coat to a pocket and produced a business card.

'I'll be in touch,' he said.

I touched my pockets. 'I didn't think to bring a card, sorry.'

The icy stare was back along with the almost smile. 'Don't worry, *chommie*,' he said, 'I know exactly how to find you.'

He started to walk off, then turned back and said, 'That security break-in at my office? Were you already keeping tabs on me?'

I was surprised. 'No, mate, sheer coincidence. Another case entirely.' He nodded, but didn't look wholly convinced.

It was probably time to contact Bronwen and start to mend fences but I held back. Best to wait until I heard something from Keppler. I drove to Erskineville to pay Ronny a visit. I was asked to wait and show ID at reception while the person in charge consulted a list.

'That's all right, Mr Hardy,' she said. 'You can go up.'

'What's happening here?'

'Mr Saunders has been assigned a guard and I have a list of people permitted to see him.'

Barry on the job, I thought. The guard was youngish, fit-looking. He got up from the hard chair he was sitting on and offered his hand.

'Rob Silvani, Mr Hardy.'

We shook. 'How's our boy?'

'Having a tough time, but he's hanging in there. Plays a mean game of five hundred.'

'You should see him in a boxing ring. Okay for me to go in?'

For an answer he opened the door before sitting down again. Ronny, in blue and white checked pyjamas, was propped up in bed watching television. When he saw me he pressed a button on a panel connected to the set by a slender cable and turned the TV off.

'Gidday, Cliff. Dad tells me I've got you to thank for hauling me out of that bloody place and getting me in here.'

'I had some help. How're you doing?'

He shook his head. 'Nightmares, and I get the shakes. They filled me full of some kind of dope.'

I sat at the end of the bed and watched him drink some water. Sweat had broken out on his forehead and he mopped at it with a tissue.

'The . . . the girl . . .'

'She's all right. She's got some money from Barry and last I heard she was headed for Queensland.'

'What about that big bastard that grabbed me? Christ. He could hit.'

'I saw the bruises. I managed to get the better of him in a more or less fair fight. He's around somewhere but I don't think you have to worry about him. Just concentrate on getting better. Are you on drugs of any sort?'

He shook his head. 'Not recently. A bit when I was

younger—that's when I got done for possession—but not the hard stuff. Bit of a binge drinker now and again, that's all.'

I nodded. 'You make a great pair, you and Barry. You bunged up here and him in hospital.'

'How is he, really?'

'Getting better, probably depends on how well he looks after himself.'

'I could help him there.'

'Do you know why all this happened to you, Ronny?'

'I suppose to get to Dad somehow.'

'Right. Well, I'll leave you to watch TV and . . . get yourself together. By the way, you said you and your sister had no family after your mum and her bloke got killed. Was it always like that?'

He went to rub at one of the scratches on his chest and as he jerked the hand away I noticed the raw friction marks on his wrist. 'Pretty much. There was an uncle who showed up a few times. Uncle George. Dad's brother. He and my mum had a flaming row and he pissed off. Why?'

'No reason. Sally Brewer was very impressed with you inside the ropes. She'd take you on if you wanted to fight professionally.'

He smiled and touched his nose and his eyebrows. 'And end up looking like you? No offence, but no thanks.'

'Very wise,' I said.

*

The streetlights were out in the lower end of Glebe Point Road when I got back and my street was in semi-darkness, with only a few house lights showing. I parked and got out, stretching and massaging an aching back. I realised how tense I'd been in my encounter with Keppler and the short drive to and from Erskineville hadn't helped. It was Sunday night and King Street was packed with people coming to the many Vietnamese and Thai restaurants that had started to spring up. I'd had to brake several times to avoid pedestrians and cars jumping the lights.

I waited until my eyes adjusted to the gloom and walked up to my gate. I groped in the letterbox and grabbed what felt like a bunch of junk mail. I juggled it with my keys in one hand and opened the gate with the other. In the dark I stumbled over one of the uplifted tiles on the path.

'Stay right there, Hardy, you cunt. Just like that.'

No mistaking the voice—Des O'Malley. A torch beam hit me and I blinked, half blinded, but I saw enough to make out the thrust of a sawn-off, double-barrelled shotgun. O'Malley was in the shadows on my porch. Perfect range for such a weapon.

'Don't do anything silly, Des.'

'I'm gonna do what I should've done a fucking long time ago.'

Just then the streetlights came back on. I threw the handful of junk mail at him and tried to get the .38 from my pocket but he batted the paper away and stepped forward quickly so that he had the shottie only a yard away from my chest.

'Say goodbye, Hardy.'

I heard a movement behind me and thought it was going to be the last thing I'd ever hear. I didn't see my life flashing before my eyes but there was a roaring in my ears before a crisp voice broke through.

'Police. O'Malley, drop the weapon.'

He didn't: he swung it to avoid me and aim at the voice but two shots followed in rapid succession and he collapsed. The shotgun hit the path and exploded, spraying its deadly load into the unkempt scrubby bushes in my garden. Lights came on and doors crashed open. I sagged against the fence as Bronwen, two hands still on her pistol, let out a low moan.

'Oh, Jesus,' she whispered. 'I think I've killed him.'

part three

25

She hadn't killed him. One of her shots had hit his right shoulder and the other smashed his right elbow. Des's right-hand punching days were done. He'd sustained a concussion when he fell and he'd bled all over my porch.

We learned this over the next few hours of madness while paramedics, cops and neighbours swarmed about. I'd gone inside to make the calls while Bron had waited with O'Malley. The paramedics stabilised him and took him away. The uniforms guarded the scene until the Glebe detectives arrived. I knew one of them but not on a friendly basis.

Bron produced Federal Police ID and surrendered her Glock. The detectives bagged the shotgun and we went in separate cars to Glebe police station. In all the ruckus I'd scarcely had time to thank Bron and she'd brushed off what I said anyway.

'I'm glad you didn't kill him,' I said.

'Why?'

'He's our ace in the hole, or one of our aces. If I can get him to confirm who hired him to take Ronny—and tell me why.'

She looked at me uncomprehendingly and we had no more time to talk. We were taken to separate rooms in the station and I had a long, solitary wait while phones rang and doors opened and closed and footsteps came and went. Eventually a man who identified himself as Detective Sergeant Luther Reiss from the Serious Crimes Unit came in with two cups of coffee. It was past midnight and he looked tired but not too unhappy. The room was set up to record an interview and he fiddled with the equipment after giving me the coffee.

He switched the recording device on and gave his name, the date, time and place and identified me. The red light glowed and I could hear faint tape hiss. He offered to wait until I had legal representation.

'No need,' I said. 'I was a victim, potentially.'

'Can you explain what happened?'

I told him O'Malley and I had a long-standing enmity and we'd come into conflict recently over matters to do with Barry Bartlett. When he asked for details I declined to give them. When he asked about Federal Police officer Bronwen Marr, I said she was part of the same deal and that I hoped she'd get a commendation for saving my life.

'I doubt it,' he said and looked sorry he'd put the comment on the record.

'Don't worry, Luther,' I said. 'You can always edit that out.'

He announced a pause and switched the machine off. 'I'd like to edit you out altogether, Hardy, but as it happens your fuck-up just might be useful.'

I knew what he meant. His assignment was the murder of Sir Keith Mountjoy by sawn-off shotgun and now he had something to work with. I looked blank and didn't say a word. He resumed the recording of the interview but it went nowhere and his heart wasn't really in it. He escorted me to the exit. I stopped and addressed the desk officer.

'What happened to the woman who was brought in with me?'

The officer looked at Reiss who nodded.

'I believe she was taken to Canberra,' he said.

All this was in the days before social media and people didn't have mobile phones to record everything happening around them. O'Malley's shooting got some newspaper and radio coverage, but there was no filmed footage. I was described as a 'Glebe resident' and O'Malley as 'a person known to police'. At the scene the local cops had kept neighbours and sticky-beaks at a distance and had quickly ushered Bron into a car. A couple of reports followed about a person being interviewed by police in hospital, but there was no further identification. Unless you knew more about it, there was no way to connect the incident with the death of Sir Keith Mountjoy.

Barry Bartlett and Ronny did know of course and they grilled me closely when I visited them a few times over the following days. Barry had studied the reports in detail and formed his own conclusion based on them and my demeanour.

'You didn't shoot Des, did you?'

'No.'

'I'm guessing it was that female cop you brought in here.'

'Why would you guess that?'

'Reading between the bloody lines. The cops're clamped right down on it the way they do when it's one of their own. Plus she had the look.'

'The look?'

'Something about her, mate.'

'You're a psychologist now, are you?'

'I know people. I twigged her as ambitious. Maybe a bit out of her depth but probably ready to step up if she had to.'

He'd read her better than me and deserved to know how things stood. I told him I thought Betty Lee Mountjoy had hired O'Malley—through the Botany Security outfit—to grab Ronny, and raised the possibility that O'Malley had offed Sir Keith.

'Jesus, so he really went rogue. I thought I was treating him okay.'

'She must've made him an offer he couldn't refuse, at least about grabbing Ronny. Whether she put a contract on Sir Keith's still up in the air.'

'Wouldn't put it past her. She's a right bitch. Ever met her?'

'No. Spoke to her on the phone once.'

'Keep it like that. She's poison.'

I explained my plan to use Keppler to get information about the Mogul insider or insiders and to do a deal with the Feds that'd involve immunity for him.

'Pretty neat,' he said. 'You're a cunning bastard.'

'But it hinges on her; Bronwen with the look,' I said.

Barry, seeming better still but tiring now, heaved himself up for more comfort against the pillows. 'She'll be back,' he said.

Ronny wasn't recovering as well as Barry; he'd apparently had a relapse since I'd last visited. The doctor told me he was suffering from shock as much as from the combined effects of drugs and alcohol.

'There's sexual trauma as well,' he said.

'Sexual trauma?'

'I gather he was subjected to some pretty extreme sado-masochistic procedures that have left a mark on him. He has nightmares about this, and we've got him sedated on Valium.'

'But he'll be okay?'

'Yes, with time and care and . . . I hesitate to say it, positive experiences.'

Didn't sound like the time to tell Ronny that Barry wasn't his dad, or that the Federal Police had tried to lay a honey

PETER CORRIS

trap for him. I went into his room and found him staring at the TV with the sound muted.

'What's on?'

'Dunno. Some dumb movie.' He clicked the remote device and turned the set off. He rubbed at the chafe marks on his wrists, now scabbing over nicely and probably itchy as hell. I'd thought they were from O'Malley's restraints and maybe they were, but, from what the doctor had said, something else as well. He reached down to the floor and pulled up a tabloid newspaper.

'You live in Glebe, don't you?'

I nodded.

'That shooting. Was it you?'

I shook my head. 'A cop shot Des O'Malley. He was after me for knocking him about when I rescued you. As they say, he's helping them with their enquiries.'

'Into what?'

I shrugged.

'There's a hell of a lot you're not telling me.'

'You have to concentrate on getting better. Barry's going to need you.'

'I'm no fucking good to him as I am. Cliff, do you remember that woman who picked me up at the drinks party?'

Careful now, I thought. *He seemed to have forgotten about her helping in Glebe and getting him to the rest home. Was he that scrambled?* 'I'm not sure . . .'

218

'I saw you pointing me out to her.'

'Oh, yeah—tall, glasses.'

'That's right. Do you know who she is?'

I shook my head. 'Who did she say she was?'

'That's the bugger of it. I can't remember after all that's happened. I really liked her and I was shitty to her, I remember that. I'd like to see her again and apologise. You're a detective. There must be a list of people invited to the party. Do you think you could find her?'

Great, I thought, *just what the doctor ordered, but tricky as hell.* 'I could try.'

He looked more alert. 'Would you? I'd be bloody grateful. I can't pay you though, and after all you've done, I . . .'

'Don't worry,' I said, 'I'm still working for your dad.'

And, I thought, *digging myself a deeper and deeper emotional hole.*

He pulled himself more upright in the bed. 'Tell you what, there's a gym here. How about we put the gloves on and have a spar?'

'Jesus, Ronny, you must be joking!'

'You look pretty fit to me and you've got a stone and a half advantage. A middleweight against the light-heavy. Come on, just a spar. I'd go easy.'

'What about your ribs?'

'Feeling better and I'll pad up. You avoid body shots and I'll stay away from that black eye.'

'Some spar that'd be. I wouldn't want anyone to see it.'

He was lively, jumping out of his skin. The Valium didn't seem to be doing much for his jitters. 'It'll be fun. Maybe you could find that . . . whatever her name is and bring her along.'

'When you're better,' I said. 'When you're out of here.'

'You're on!' he shouted.

At home I put together a rather wilted salad, grilled some chops and boiled some new potatoes that weren't really new anymore. I put Dylan's *Desire* on the stereo and ate while listening to 'Hurricane'. Great song, great album. I was down to the last few chords and mouthfuls when the phone rang. I gulped, swilled and answered.

'Hardy, I think you know who this is.'

Keppler. I resisted the mischievous impulse to imitate his accent.

'Yes.'

'I may have some names for you,' Keppler said.

'That's interesting. You'll have to give me some time to make arrangements.'

'There's no hurry. I see your adversary O'Malley is in hospital. Under guard, would you say?'

'I imagine so.'

'Lucky for him, however it turns out. There's no hurry but don't leave it too long before contacting me.'

'What's too long?'

'I'll leave that to your imagination.'

He hung up. He was no fool, Keppler. I was left in no doubt about his potential for ruthless action and the essential vulnerability of my position. But it cut both ways; he would be equally edgy, and I calculated I had time to figure out how to contact Bron and the *Federales*.

26

As it turned out I didn't have to bother. When I checked the answering machine there was a message, in a muffled voice that might or might not have been Bron's. 'Call BM,' followed by a phone number. The big question was whether this was a private message or Bronwen contacting me in her official police capacity. I found myself hoping it was both, although I was unsure how that would work. I rang the number.

'Yes?' Her voice.

'Bron, it's Cliff.'

'Good. We have to talk.'

'What about?'

She ignored that. 'What have you been doing?'

'Just now? Sparring with Ronny Saunders about not sparring with him.'

'What?'

'You asked, I told you.'

'You're an infuriating man. I mean . . .'

'I know what you mean and I need to talk to you, but I have to know who I'm talking to, a private person or a member of the Federal Police. I'll talk to either but I need to know first.'

'Why?'

'Because I've made some progress and I need official help. If they've kicked you out of the force, well, we can go out for a meal and see what happens. If you're still working I need to see you urgently. That is, after I see some evidence that you're still on the job.'

'What kind of evidence?'

'A colleague with credentials.'

There was a long pause while she digested this. Eventually I heard an exasperated sigh. 'That can be arranged,' she said. 'Be at my flat at 10 am tomorrow.'

'Please,' I said.

She laughed. 'Cliff . . .'

'Do I bring a plate?'

'Bring whatever you like, just be there. How's Ronald?'

'Getting better. He wants to see you to apologise for his bad behaviour the night he wanted to fuck you.'

'Does he know that you and I . . . ?'

'No. He doesn't even remember that you were there to clean him up and help get him to the rest home. That's how out of it he was.'

'Is he part of this progress you say you've made?' I could

hear the reluctance to ask in her voice but her need to do it. I thought that was enough for now.

'No, it's something else,' I said. 'See you tomorrow.'

I hung up and thought things over. Barry and Ronny were safe; Des O'Malley was out of the way; Keppler was being cooperative and it looked as if I had made contact with the Federal Police. Bronwen had laughed. Why didn't I feel better?

I caught sight of my reflection in the heavy glass door to Bronwen's block of flats. I looked tired. The door clicked open in response to the buzzer and I went up to her floor. I knocked and Bronwen let me in. No hug, no kiss.

She wore a stylish grey blouse with a loose tie at the neck, a just-below-the-knee black skirt and medium heels. She escorted me into the living area where a man in a suit was standing looking out the window.

'Cliff, this is Commander Simon Black of the Federal Police. Sir, this is Cliff Hardy.'

We shook hands. Black was a medium-sized man in every sense—height, breadth, weight. He was in his mid-forties, greying at the temples, with a world-weary look. Dark suit, white shirt, blue tie. I'd dressed down—leather jacket, navy open-necked shirt, jeans, Blundstones. He didn't like the look of me and didn't like being shorter, lighter and, at a guess, having no desk to sit behind. I sat in an armchair. I might have made the move with more familiarity than I'd intended and he didn't like that either. He remained standing.

'Coffee?' Bronwen said.

Black nodded.

'Thanks, Bron,' I said, 'black no sugar.'

She went out of the room and Black took a notebook from his pocket and turned over a few leaves. 'Sergeant Marr has you saying you've made progress. I assume that means in relation to the investigation she's told you about.'

His tone betrayed his intense unhappiness that she'd told me anything. I shifted for more comfort in the chair and looked past him out at the grey sky.

'Did she also tell you that I want to see solid evidence that you are who you are and hold the rank she says you do?'

'You don't trust her?'

'Jesse James trusted Bob Ford, and look what happened there.'

His dislike of me intensified but he took out his wallet and passed me an embossed photo ID card and a letter from the head of the Federal Police Force advising him of his promotion to his present rank. I handed the documents back.

'Do you expect me to call you Commander?'

He unbuttoned his jacket and dropped into the chair opposite me. 'Hardy, you can call me whatever the fuck you like as long as you stop playing games and get serious.'

'You're right, Simon,' I said. 'I was just sizing you up. Serious it is, but I think Sergeant Marr should be present.'

Bron came in with a tray, a coffee pot, three mugs, milk and sugar. She sat on the sofa, served herself and left us to do the same.

I told them about my suspicions that Betty Lee Mountjoy had hired O'Malley to snatch Ronny to use against his father. The look they exchanged indicated that they registered the irony of this. It had been their own plan, minus the kidnap, I assumed. I said it was possible that O'Malley had killed Sir Keith but that I had no solid evidence of that. I said that O'Malley's attempt to kill me was a private matter between us and that Sergeant Marr had saved my life. I added that I had a possible source who might confirm what I thought.

'A source?' Black said. 'You're talking like a bloody journalist.'

'Worst enemy of you covert types,' I said. 'A go-between, then—a player—the person who says he has some names to give us. People inside the Mogul refinery who could be the operators of the scam you're investigating.'

That got their attention. Black had been sipping his coffee and not displaying a lot of interest until this point. He put his mug down as I picked mine up for dramatic effect.

'You say you have a . . . source inside Mogul?' Black said.

'Not inside, but close, very close. He's willing to meet you and give you the names and his evidence of their . . . complicity.'

'Who is this?'

I finished my coffee and sat back. I shot a look at Bronwen, who was studying her hands.

'There's some dealing to be done before we get to that,' I said. 'I'm hoping you have the authority to make these deals.'

'Money?'

'No.'

I told them about the need for immunity from prosecution for Barry Bartlett and my source.

Black shook his head. 'Bartlett's a major target.'

'He's not *the* major target and you're getting nowhere. You don't know who the major target is.'

'And you do?'

'I think so. It all needs a bit more work and that can only be done if you agree to my terms.'

'What's to stop us arresting you and charging you with obstruction and possibly a few other things?'

'You'll never get close to the heart of it if you do.'

'This . . . informant of yours, what crimes of his have to be overlooked?'

'Just involvement in the kidnapping of Ronald Saunders, as far as I know. I should have said that Bartlett will cooperate with you in return for immunity.'

Black twisted his wedding ring several times. 'That does put a different light on it. I think I can ensure the immunities if the information leads to a prosecution.'

I shook my head. 'Too many legal and political slip-ups possible in that. I need something more solid up-front.'

Black got up, stretched and stood staring out of the window. I looked at Bronwen. She shrugged, and I had no idea what that meant.

Eventually Black turned around to face me.

'Under certain circumstances the Attorney-General can give a written guarantee of immunity as long as the testimony of the person concerned is utterly truthful.'

'That sounds very legalistic. Are you a lawyer?'

'I was.'

'That'd be okay for Barry but ... my source won't be testifying at all and he's the one with the crucial information.'

'If I understand you,' Bronwen spoke slowly and deliberately as if distilling everything she'd heard so far, 'his crime is just to do with the ... abduction of Ronald. Arranging, not actually conducting it.'

I nodded.

'His evidence could be given in camera and taped and we could give an undertaking that would also be taped. Perhaps a transcript of that could even be signed and lodged somewhere mutually agreeable.'

'That'd do it,' I said.

'Of course,' Black said, 'alternatively we could subpoena your telephone records and find out who you've been talking to.'

I smiled at him. 'That wouldn't help you. But if you've got CCTV cameras installed in Jubilee Park, Glebe ...'

Bronwen's grin was cut off by a glance from Black. 'It was just a thought,' Black said. 'Sergeant, would you be so kind as to get my coat? I've got a lot to do.'

Bronwen came back with a dark coat and a blue scarf. Black shrugged into the coat and arranged the scarf fussily.

'I'll be in touch through Sergeant Marr,' he said. 'There'll have to be a number of meetings, you understand.'

I was on my feet, politely. 'Yeah,' I said, 'meetings to arrange meetings.'

'Precisely.'

He gave me a curt nod and Bronwen escorted him out. I moved quickly across to the door to listen for any conversation between them in the hallway outside but if there was one, it was too brief and quiet for me to hear. I was taking off my jacket in the now overheated room when Bronwen came back. She stood, fiddling with the tie at the neck of her blouse.

'He didn't ask for any evidence that I actually have a source,' I said.

'Do you have evidence?'

'Just a scrap.'

'He's not dumb, Cliff. If you were bluffing you're the greatest actor since Olivier.'

I tried for the Welsh plus Oxford voice: 'Burton, for mine, darling.'

We moved simultaneously, wrapped our arms around each other and kissed fiercely.

*

Later, between the sheets, I asked her what had happened after she'd shot O'Malley. She said she'd been taken to Canberra and thoroughly grilled over everything that had gone on since her assignment to contact Ronny.

'And you told them everything?'

'Yes, my career was on the line.'

It was warm in the bed and we'd both had big slugs of brandy in fresh coffees. I liked the long length of her next to me. I stroked her bare shoulders. She kissed me and let her hand slide up my leg to my crotch.

'Go ahead, ask questions. I won't be offended.'

'I don't want to ask questions.'

'Yes you do.'

'All right, did they . . . exonerate you?'

'Yes.'

'And what's your assignment now?'

She laughed. 'To keep an eye on you and get as much out of you as I can.'

'Well, you've done that.'

'Have I?'

'For now.'

She kissed me again. 'I'm glad I didn't fuck Ronald.'

'So am I,' I said. 'But quite a few others did.'

27

We decided to visit Ronny. I told Bron again that he wanted to apologise to her.

'That'd be nice,' she said, 'I can't remember when I last had an apology.'

'Don't get a lot of that in our game,' I said.

'*Our* game? I like that.'

We took the Audi and didn't speak much on the drive, didn't need to; we'd reached that point of companionship that feels good but which I'd learned to mistrust. When we arrived at the rest home the receptionist looked at me with a puzzled frown.

'We'd like to see Mr Saunders,' I said.

'He's gone, Mr Hardy.'

'He's what?'

'He left this morning with the man who was guarding him. Let me see, a Mr Bartlett rang and settled the bill by credit card. The . . . guard had clothes for Mr Saunders.'

'What did Dr Richardson say?'

She became flustered at my sharpness. 'He wasn't on duty. There was nothing I could do, Mr Hardy. Mr Saunders was a voluntary patient and the account had been settled by a man who said he was his father. Mr Saunders had showed great improvement after . . .'

'Yes, yes. It's not your fault.'

She scrabbled on her desk and came up with an envelope. 'This was left for you. I thought everything was a bit abrupt and I wondered about the medications but . . .'

I almost snatched the envelope from her and turned away. Bron watched me tear it open and we reached a moment of truth. I read the message and handed the sheet of paper to her. Block capitals read: GO TO YOUR OFFICE CHECK FAX.

'Better do it,' Bron said. 'Am I in this with you or not?'

I nodded to the receptionist, took Bron's arm and we hurried out. We moved quickly to the Audi, got in and Bron started the motor.

'What do you think?' she said.

'I'm trying to work it out. St Peters Lane, Darlinghurst. Fast as you can.'

'Who was this guard?'

'Barry assigned a guard. I don't know who he used for a job of this kind but I've got a horrible feeling I'm about to find out.'

'This is something you haven't told us about.'

'Sorry. I think it's to do with my informant. It should become clearer when I've read the fax.'

The silence on this drive was of a different order. My mind was buzzing with possibilities, none of which had any real substance. But a gut feeling can overrun substance. After a while I abandoned all thought apart from a concern for Ronny, who could never have imagined the things that were in store for him when he left the Old Dart.

Bron parked in my space and we went up to the office. She wasn't impressed by the surroundings and sneezed as some of the disturbed age-old dust hit her. I was used to it. I opened the door and went straight to the fax machine. A sheet had spilled out and fallen into the tray. It was a dark, blotchy photograph of a hooded man tied to a chair. A sleeve of his shirt had been ripped away to expose a tattoo.

Ronny.

Bron looked enquiringly at me and I nodded. At the bottom of the photo a phone number was written in thick black ink. I took out Keppler's card and showed it to Bron.

'This is your source?'

I nodded.

'And you let him grab Ronald.'

'Not exactly. Hold on.'

The light on my answering machine was blinking and I hit the play button. Barry's voice, strangled, agitated, crackled.

'Cliff, what the fuck's going on? I got a call telling me to settle Ronny's bill or he'd be dead. Whoever it was put Ronny on and he said he had a knife at his throat, so I did it. Where the fuck are you? What're you doing?'

I rang Barry's number and put the phone on broadcast. Barry answered and shouted abuse.

'Shut up, Barry. Who did you use to provide guards for Ronny?'

'What? Shit, that Botany Security mob. I . . .'

'Okay, take it easy. They won't kill him. They want to bargain.'

'Who? I don't fuckin' understand.'

'You will. Take it easy. Take a pill. I've gotta go.'

I hung up. I sat in my chair behind the desk and pulled the phone towards me. Bron perched on the edge of the desk and lit a cigarette, the first I'd ever seen her smoke. I felt like one myself, but after several smoke-free years I fought the urge.

She smoked and tapped ash into the waste-paper bin. 'So?'

I told her about Keppler and him undertaking to help the investigation of the Mogul scam in return for immunity. I said he'd told me he had names and I said that I thought a meeting between him and her Commander Black and Barry might help resolve things to everyone's satisfaction.

'You took a lot on yourself,' she said.

'Too much.' I dialled the number on the fax sheet. As expected, after a few bleeps—Keppler.

'Hardy, it's time for you to take stock.'

'How's that?'

'You've been talking to the Federal Police.'

'That was the arrangement.'

'The arrangement has changed. I'm no longer seeking immunity for supposed crimes. In fact, I never was. Just wanted to see how much you wanted the information. Surprised you fell for it, Hardy—thought you'd be more suspicious.'

'Actual crimes,' I said. 'Not "supposed".' I was trying to get the upper hand—he was right. I should have been more suspicious.

'As you wish. You're going to call the Federal Police off. You're going to tell them you were bluffing, or lying about having information. I don't care which.'

'Why would I do that?'

'You've seen the photograph. That young man is our bargaining chip.'

'It's too late, Keppler. I've already told them about my conversation with you.'

'No you haven't.'

Bron's eyebrows shot up when she heard that. I put my finger to my lips.

'There's no hurry,' Keppler said. 'We'll hold our young hostage to ensure Mr Bartlett's silence while you persuade your girlfriend to . . . let us say, divert the investigation. Point it in another direction.'

'I'm not sure I can do that.'

'You must.'

'Or what?'

'Or young Mr Saunders dies and in such a way that it appears you've killed him.'

'Nonsense.'

'It's not nonsense, *chommie*. We have the resources to do it. I'll leave you to think it over.'

'Let me speak to him.'

'No.'

He hung up. I replaced the receiver, pulled out the deep bottom drawer and fished out the bottle of scotch, half full; or half empty, depending on your mood. Paper cups from another drawer, ice from the bar fridge. I looked at Bron, who'd moved from the desk to the client chair. She stubbed her cigarette in the waste-paper bin and was lighting another.

'Is that your solution?' she said.

I fanned smoke away, although there really wasn't much. 'Is that yours?'

I made two strong drinks and pushed one towards her.

'This is a mess,' she said.

'It's a cock-up, is what it is,' I said. 'Partly theirs—' I pointed to the fax sheet—'partly mine, partly yours.'

We each had a drink. She snuffed out the barely smoked cigarette. 'How do you figure that?'

'I should've checked on the guard, found out who he worked for. I shouldn't have taken so much of what Keppler said at face value.'

'Okay. I can see that. What mistake has he made?'

I had another drink and re-ran Keppler's words in my mind. 'The stakes have gone up. He's talked to someone he's working with.'

'Who?'

'I'd be guessing.'

'So, guess.'

'He's more involved in the fuel scam than I thought. That was dumb of me. That's one thing. I think he might also be more involved in the Keith Mountjoy hit.'

'You didn't say much about that to Commander Black.'

I shrugged. 'It was all paper-thin at that point, but I wondered if Lady Mountjoy had two commissions for O'Malley.'

'So what are you wondering now?'

'I'm wondering if the dragon lady is also right in the middle of the fuel scam, up to her neck in it, and Keppler is providing big-time protection.'

Bron swilled her drink. 'I met her briefly at the BBE bash.'

'How did she strike you?'

'As expensive and . . . influential.'

I nodded and we both drank slowly. Some of the tension went out of her as the liquor worked. She slumped a little in the chair. 'You don't need to spell it out.'

'Spell what out?'

'Your suspicions as far as our unit is concerned,' she said. 'The way we haven't made much progress. The feeling that we're off the pace somehow. Some of us believe we've got a leak.'

I shook my head. 'You haven't got a leak, love, I think you've got a mole.'

28

Bron said there were six members of the special unit, including herself. I asked her if there was anyone she thought could be a candidate.

'That's hard,' she said. 'It's hard to make a difference between dislike and distrust.'

'Black?'

'No, he's a straight arrow, I'm sure.'

'If you had to guess.'

She finished her drink and crushed the paper cup. 'Courtney Beal,' she said in a perfect harsh Boston accent. Very Katharine Hepburn.

'American?'

'Very. I'll bet her underwear has stars and stripes on it. She was seconded from FBI, part of our suck-up to our nearest and dearest ally program. She's a creep.'

'Glad to see you're not differentiating between dislike and distrust.'

'You asked. She comes on to all the men, never does anything really, but never puts a foot wrong.'

'Do you know anything else about her?'

'Only that she's got all the tickets. Degree from Duke, MBA from Harvard.'

'How old is she?'

Bron caught the sudden rise in the level of my interest. 'Late thirties. Why?'

'Lady Betty Lee Mountjoy did her MBA at Harvard.'

'That's thin.'

'Let's try and thicken it up. Let's say Lady Betty Lee is the money and the brains behind the whole thing and Keppler is in it with her and your Courtney Beal is their mole.'

'That's a massive set of assumptions.'

'It fits certain facts.' I gestured for her to come and sit in my chair with the phone to hand. I got up and took Keppler's card from my wallet.

'That's your bit of evidence,' Bron said.

'Right. You ring him and use that voice you do so well. Just say who you are. If he recognises the voice and reacts, he'll be angry because presumably they'd have a different way of communicating, certainly not the number on his card.'

She cleared her throat. 'Okay, then what?'

'You just sound agitated, apologise, and say you'll call again later and hang up.'

'If you're right about this he'll contact her.'

'Yes, and she'll deny calling him and . . .'

'He won't believe her and he'll be worried.'

'I would be,' I said. 'Shit!'

'What?'

'Nearly a fatal mistake. He'll have caller ID and he knows my number. We'll have to do it from a public phone. Better in a way—traffic noise'll help. Are you sure you can do it, Bron?'

'You're a bit of a mimic yourself, aren't you?'

'Whitlam of course, Burton, Bogart, Michael Caine, that's about it.'

'I'm a bit more versatile than that and I've got that bitch down pat.'

We left the office and found a phone just inside a shop in William Street. The traffic was loud but not thunderous. I gave Bron the card and she dialled the number. I couldn't hear Keppler's response but she went through the routine pretty much as I'd suggested it. She kissed the card before handing it back to me.

'Like clockwork. He'll be a worried man. What now?'

'You convince Commander Black that we're on to something and bring him in with all the resources he can muster.'

We walked back to St Peters Lane and her car. She jiggled her keys and let out a sigh.

I took her arm. 'What?'

'I forgot all about Ronald.'

'I didn't. We have no idea where he is and this is the only way I can think of to find him.'

We went to Bron's flat and she phoned Commander Black. I went out onto the balcony to let her talk in private. I had a sense that she needed to demonstrate some independence and I was happy to give her room for that.

She came out and stood beside me as a nippy wind buffeted the city. Spring in Sydney, before global warming started to bite. I put my arm around her shoulders. She didn't resist but she didn't draw any closer.

'He's coming,' she said.

'You must have been convincing.'

'I think he dislikes Ms Beal as much as I do. All we can do is lay it out for him and see what action he's prepared to take.'

When I didn't reply she dug an elbow into my ribs.

'What're you thinking, Cliff?'

'I'm wondering whether it wouldn't be better for me just to get to Keppler and apply the blowtorch.'

'I don't think so. I think we have to bargain with him to save Ronald. I feel sort of responsible for him.'

We went inside when rain slanted into the balcony. Still standing close beside me, Bron asked me if I wanted a drink.

'What've you got?'

'Beer and scotch.'

'I'll have a little of both. Does the Commander like a drink?'

'I don't know. We've never socialised.'

'Doesn't sound like a cosy operational unit.'

'It isn't. It never jelled. Always full of tension. The original idea was that Beal would go after Ronald but she somehow managed to hive it off to me. It was a shitty assignment; that's why I feel responsible for him.'

Ronny had been drawn into the trouble by other forces, but the sentiment did her credit. She produced a bottle of Bell's and a long-neck Resch's pilsener and put them on the coffee table with glasses and a bowl of ice cubes.

'Go for your life,' she said.

The doorbell rang. Bron answered it and ushered Black, shrugging out of his coat, into the room. He saw the bottles on the table and nodded to Bron.

'A large scotch and water please, Bronwen. Evening, Hardy. I'm gritting my teeth to try not to call you a fucking cowboy.'

'Call me what you like, but your little mob got nowhere at all and now we at least have some idea of who's involved in this thing.'

He nodded his thanks to Bron for the drink and took a long pull on it. 'Bronwen told me just enough to get me here. I want the two of you to go over it all in detail and convince me that I did the right thing.'

Bron and I talked for some time, interrupting and glossing each other, and spelling out our slender evidence and strong suspicions. Black sipped his drink and remained silent. The rain drummed on the glass doors to the balcony. Relaxed by the whisky, Black and I took off our jackets. Bron looked cool and collected in her silk blouse but she toyed with the tie at the neck and I knew she desperately wanted a cigarette.

When we'd finished, Black drained his glass, reached out and made himself a weaker drink.

'It might surprise you to know, Hardy, that we had suspicions of Lady Mountjoy.'

'But not of Richard Keppler or Courtney Beal,' I said.

'No. Assuming you're right, we have two targets. I'm empowered to arrest them both.'

'Better do it quickly, sir,' Bron said. 'Otherwise Cliff is proposing to act . . . unilaterally.'

Black sipped at his diluted scotch. 'Is he really? That raises interesting possibilities.'

29

Never underestimate a bureaucrat. The smart ones have a thousand ways to shift the blame to someone else and claim any credit that's going. They may seem to have all their energies concentrated on the job at hand, but they have their own agendas, which only become apparent later.

Black was one of those people who could turn on the charm when he wanted to and make you feel he was doing you a favour when he proposed something. He outlined a strategy that involved me confronting Keppler and offering him a deal—no prosecution in return for everything he knew about the fuel operation including names and documentation, plus the release of Ronald Saunders unharmed. It was more or less the arrangement I thought I'd worked out with Keppler, with one difference. Black would move against Lady Betty Lee Mountjoy with all the resources at his command but delay just long enough for Keppler to agree to the terms.

'It's a tried and tested method,' Black said. 'It's called leverage.' He pronounced it the American way. 'Keppler knows that Lady Mountjoy would drop everyone in the shit to save her own skin. He has to take the deal before she can do that.'

It sounded as though Black had bought our story lock, stock and barrel but I wasn't convinced.

'Would that be a bluff on your part about Lady Betty Lee?'

'It would be up to you to convince Keppler that it isn't.'

That wasn't an answer but it was clearly all I was going to get. Black said he'd have a team to back me up when I made my run at Keppler.

'What about Beal?' Bron said.

Black smiled and finished his drink. 'Leave her to me,' he said.

The arrangement was for me to present myself at Botany Security at 4 pm the following day and demand to see Keppler in private. Black would arrange for an interruption to the office's electricity supply and put two of his people, acting as technicians, inside the building.

'We'll have studied the floor plans and put them as close to you as possible,' Black said. 'How personally dangerous is Keppler, would you say?'

I thought about that solid build, the calm, the steely eyes. 'Very.' I didn't mention I'd already seen the floor plans.

'You'll be armed, I take it?'

'I'll think about it.'

'I would.'

We left it there. Black said he'd organise a meeting with all parties for 2 pm the next day at his hotel in Bondi. He had a brief private conversation with Bron in the hall before he left. When she came back she looked anxious.

'Are you worried or just hungry?' I said.

'Fuck you, this is no joke. What do you think about this plan?'

I shrugged. 'It's full of holes, but I can't think of anything better. Can you?'

'No. I just wish there was some way we could find out where Ronald is. Some other way, I mean.'

'We got lucky last time, now it's different. Keppler could have him stashed anywhere.'

She paced the room. 'I know. I studied that fax. There's absolutely no hint as to where the picture was taken.'

'Keppler's not dumb.'

She stopped pacing and came close. 'And he's dangerous.'

I put my arms around her. 'So am I, Sergeant. Let's go out and eat.'

Seven people gathered in Black's suite at the Bondi Regent—Black, me and five Federal Police officers. Introductions were brief and not overly friendly. Which of them were actually members of Black's unit and which had been seconded from elsewhere I didn't know or care. Two were in convincing-looking electricity technician overalls. Black spent nearly an hour outlining how it would go down. They would go inside the building just before me; the others would take up support positions nearby. Each of them would communicate with Black via the sorts of electronic systems that require an earpiece. The 'technicians' could credibly claim they were getting relevant information from headquarters.

I had a sense that not all the cops were happy with the arrangement and particularly with my involvement. Black had the floor plan of the Botany Security building and pointed out the largest of the rooms, two doors along from where the receptionist sat.

'That has to be for the boss,' he said.

'Where's Sergeant Marr?' I asked Black. 'Shouldn't she be in on this in some way?'

'She is,' Black said and wouldn't volunteer anything more. He turned to gaze out at the rain and one of the men in overalls took me aside and asked if I was armed. I showed him the .38.

'I hear you and Bronwen are an item.'

I nodded.

'She's bloody good,' he said. 'I don't know why she isn't here. Anyway, you strike trouble, you fire a shot and we'll come running.'

Black went over the plan again, such as it was. We

synchronised our watches at Black's insistence and we were off to Little Bay, me in my car, the 'technicians' in a van bearing an electrical services logo and the rest in nondescript sedans. As I drove I was full of apprehension. The team was far from united and, unless my eyes deceived me, every one of them, apart from Black, had some kind of body armour under their overalls and shirts.

I pulled into a parking space marked VISITORS beside the Botany Security building. I went up the steps and through the heavy glass door to where a female receptionist in a slightly military-looking suit sat at a desk.

'Yes, sir?'

'I want to see Dick, Dick Keppler.'

The use of the diminutive startled her as I'd hoped it would. 'Mr Keppler? Do you have . . . ?'

'Fuck that! I know where his office is. Just tell him I'm coming.'

She stood and moved as if to block my way. 'Who . . . ?'

'Cliff,' I shouted as I brushed past her and headed down the corridor. The second door on the right had Keppler's name on it and his title of Director. I pushed it open and went inside slamming it behind me. Keppler looked up, the change in his usually set, controlled features registering his surprise.

'Hardy, you can't just . . .'

I dropped into the chair across from his desk. 'Yes I can. This is a different ball game. I've been dealing with the Federal Police.'

He was back in control. 'How astonishing.'

Sitting forward belligerently, I told him that I could definitely offer him immunity from prosecution in return for information and the release of Ronny.

He heard me out with no interruption or any visible reaction. His hands remained still on the surface of his desk and his eyes never left my face. This was a man assured of what he was doing and comfortable in his own skin. When I'd finished he shook his head.

'These are the same terms I rejected before,' he said. 'I now hold another card.'

'The game's changed, *chommie*,' I said. 'The Feds have targeted Lady Mountjoy. They'll pressure her, offer her some kind of big fish deal that won't involve you. Rather the opposite. Better to throw in with the authorities now and cut your losses.'

'That's interesting, Hardy. And quite persuasive. But there's something you haven't taken into account.'

His confidence worried me. 'And what's that?'

'Do you have any idea how much money is involved?'

I shrugged. 'What good's money when you're in gaol?'

'This kind of money makes that virtually impossible. You may think you know what's going on, but believe me, you don't. The local players, including your friend Bartlett, have been doing all right but the system that's been developed . . .' He spread his hands. 'It's worldwide, global. You're an irritant, nothing more.'

He was convincing in his complacency and I struggled to think of an effective reply. He appeared to lose interest and had begun to shuffle papers on his desk when there was a furious tapping of high heels in the corridor and the door flew open. A tall, blonde woman, stylishly dressed in a suit but dishevelled and wild-eyed, burst into the room and rushed towards Keppler. I recognised her . . . she was the woman I'd seen when I breached the place's shit security.

Her voice was a high-pitched American-accented scream. 'Richard, oh, Richard, I've killed that Marr bitch. I had to. She . . .'

She noticed me. She reached into the pocket of her coat, pulled out a pistol and pointed it at me. I was already moving and she was distraught, and her hand shook.

I lunged at her but she was too quick and fired, missing me completely. Black's two officers rushed in with guns levelled. The woman swung towards them but one of the cops shot her before she could aim.

'No!' Keppler roared. 'Courtney!' He came around the desk in a couple of strides and grappled with the shooter. The woman had sagged against the wall, still holding her pistol. I scrambled towards her but this time she managed to fire at the struggling men. The bullet hit Keppler and he collapsed. I knocked the woman's gun from her hand and the other cop covered her.

I stood. Two of us on our feet, two on the floor with the blood pooling, one moaning. Keppler was silent and still.

30

There was a long silence after I'd finished telling the much abridged story.

'Jesus Christ,' Megan said. 'What happened then?'

'Not a lot.'

'What d'you mean, not a lot? There's dead bodies everywhere and . . .'

'Keppler was right about the size of the operation and its reach, but he hadn't allowed for the human factor. Black had sent Bron after Courtney Beal and it must've all gone wrong. It was all too big ever to be really opened up. Black was hand-in-glove with the intelligence boys and some politicians. D notices went out to the media and a kind of embargo cloud settled on every aspect of the business. Corporations changed hands, new security protocols regarding petroleum refining and trading were drawn up, blah, blah.'

'Fuck that. I mean what happened to the people?'

'Like who?'

'Like all of them, you bugger.'

I told her that Bronwen Marr was posthumously decorated for having lost her life in the course of an action the details of which were protected by provisions of various national security acts.

'That's a quote.'

Megan came up and put her hands on my shoulders. I put my hands on her tight-as-a-drum belly.

'I'm sorry, Cliff.'

'Yeah. Courtney Beal was patched up and underwent treatment for mental disturbance before being shipped back to the US. Or so I was told. I was debriefed by Black but whether he told me the truth or not I never found out.'

'Who killed Sir Keith?'

'Mountjoy? Probably Des O'Malley, on Lady Betty's orders. Sir Keith had served his purpose and he was becoming a nuisance. But they never charged anyone. Ballistics can't match up shells and shot with shotguns as they can with pistols and rifles.'

'Lady Mountjoy?'

I shrugged. 'Out of the country the very day it all blew up and never returned. I read that she married someone in Singapore. I don't think he was a rickshaw driver.'

'And Ronny?'

'Never found.'

'What? You mean Keppler killed him?'

'I'd like to think so but it's unlikely. Keppler planned to use him as a bargaining chip and he'd want him alive.'

'But that means . . . ?'

I nodded. 'Keppler stashed him somewhere and he never told anyone where. The cops looked into it, but not very hard. I worked on it for a long time but I never got a hint and Barry Bartlett never spoke to me again.'